Banished From the Pack

Rejected Mate

Book One

Alexa B. James

&

Calinda B.

Chapter One

Axel

I'm balls deep in Trixie, but I can't come. I've tried everything, from domination to trying different positions, but nothing's working. And if we can't come, we can't know for sure whether we're True Mates.

We've tried tilted missionary to get her G-Spot singing. I put her in my lap, but my legs went to sleep. We explored something she called "The Amazing Bee," where she was on top, squatting, which was supposed to allow me to explore different kinds of thrusts. But Trixie said my cock kept jamming against her cervix and it hurt, so she couldn't climax.

It might seem like no great loss. After all, we're friends, but we don't love each other. We're not even particularly attracted to each other. We're here because we got to talking about True Mates, and how you could know that person, the other half of your soul, your whole life and never know they were the mate to both your wolf and your human if you never fucked them.

I have my suspicions that you'd know it somehow, that you couldn't help but feel a soul-bond even without fucking, though you might not know what it was. But you don't get a True Mate mark until you come together—literally. We were both bored and horny, so we thought we'd try it out and make sure. If it turned out we were True Mates, we'd laugh about how we were right in front of each other all along.

I've heard fucking a True Mate is like nothing else in the world, and seeing as how today we can't even reach the finish line, I'm guessing that once again, I've struck out.

It's entirely possible that I don't have a True Mate. In fact, most wolves don't. Just because I'm the Alpha of the Jacksonville pack, that doesn't increase my chances. I inherited the position, but it wasn't magically ordained. If the older wolf who challenged me soon after I took over had won, he'd be Alpha right now, not me. Fate doesn't choose a pack's Alpha.

Finally, Trixie shakes her head. "This isn't working, boss. I'm going to head home and finish up with my vibrator."

"You can use your fingers while you're here," I say, squeezing one of her little tits.

"Nah. I need a shower, anyway." She climbs off of me, and my cock lands with a sticky, wet splat against my belly. "Maybe next time."

"Sure," I say, peeling off the condom and tossing it. We both know there won't be a next time. Our connection doesn't work, just like none of the other empty lays have worked. Even when I come, it's a disappointment when I look down and find my arm unmarked, when I feel nothing but the usual release of emptying my seed. No True Mate by my side to lead the pack. No heir to take over when I'm gone.

After Trixie leaves, I pick up my phone from the chipped wood bedstand and see I missed a text. I'm thankful for the distraction—until I read the message. Then, my blood turns white-hot.

It's a text message from one of my wolf scouts, a guy named Tiva.

The vampires struck again. Six injuries. No fatalities... Yet.

I let out a low growl and snatch up my clothes. I've had just about enough of these fucking vampires. Taking a few deep breaths calms my anger. I direct a glare out the front window to my pack's wet little corner of Jacksonville, Florida.

A half-inch of water covers the road, as usual. At least we didn't get another mega-flood last night. Like many of Jacksonville's homes, the dull beige-colored house across from mine has boards over the windows. It's uninhabitable. Since my small house stands ever so slightly uphill from the houses across the street, I was spared from the last great flood. The house has miraculously remained intact despite the endless storms that hit this region, though I've spent way too damn many hours replacing shingles, shutters, and carpet.

I may be our pack's Alpha, but the bayous, swamps, and rivers are the land's true kings.

I squeeze my phone nearly to the breaking point, hoping to channel some of the rage I feel. "Fucking vampires," I mutter through gritted teeth. Fuck them and their bloodlust and lack of respect for our boundaries. Six of my pack are injured. At least no one died—*this* time.

Anger burns in my chest as I remember what happened the last time the bloodthirsty motherfuckers struck. My Second—

the wolf with whom I'd explored, romped, and played with as a pup and adventured with as an adult—was killed.

Life without Phoenix has been brutal. We were always together—fighting side by side, covering each other's back, or whooping it up in the bars at night. Now he's dead.

They're going to fucking pay.

Fully intending to storm their lair and exact justice, I shove my phone in my pocket, don my clothes, and head out of the bedroom. On the way out, I shove my feet into my leather boots and kick open the screen door.

The door whacks against the side of the house with a satisfying crash, probably shaking loose a few ash-gray flakes of paint. One of these days, I'm going to have to re-paint this house. But that day is not today. Today, I've got bloodsucker ass to kick.

"Temper, temper," comes a voice to my right.

I spin to find Ama, my new Second in Command, spread out on the porch swing, with one leg resting on the cushioned arm. Short and muscular, she reclines on the swing with her onyx hair draped over one shoulder and her left tit.

She lowers the supernatural gossip rag she's been reading and rests it in her lap. "Where you off to in such a fury?"

"The vamps struck again," I snap, fury pounding in my temples.

"Shit," Ama says, removing her leg from its comfortable position and sitting up straight. "Who's dead?" She finger-combs the long strands of hair still trailing along the front of her torso. It's a gesture she resorts to when she's agitated or nervous.

"No one, this time."

"And you're going to go kick some ass, am I right?" She stands and sashays toward me, placing her small hand on my bicep.

The too-familiar gesture makes me tense.

Ama regards me through thick black lashes. "Do you think it's wise to go off all half-cocked like this? Shouldn't you think things through?"

"You're probably right, but fuck that. I'm sick of this shit." I step back from her, and her hand drifts to her side.

She sighs the way she always does when I rebuff her affection. "You know," she begins, licking her lips. "If you'd take a mate, you'd be the strongest wolf in southeast territory. No one would fuck with our pack."

"This again." I tromp to the porch steps and lower myself onto them, with my booted feet two steps down.

The air outside is sultry and thick, like clotted cream, bringing instant sweat to my limbs and neck. Holding my head in my hands, I consider her words. Of course I need a mate. I'm already thirty, for fucks' sake. I should have mated years ago when I became Alpha of the Jacksonville pack. I just haven't found the right partner. Holding out hope for a True Mate is a romantic notion that I should have outgrown a long time ago. A True Mate is like a soul mate to a human. It's a wonderful thing, but you don't waste your life waiting for one to show up. True Mates are rare. Most of the other Alphas in the country don't have them. They chose partners who were strong, cunning, and politically connected. I need to do the same. It's long overdue.

Ama sidles over and sits next to me on the step. "You know," she says in a dulcet voice. Her fingertips trail along my forearm. "I'm available."

I withdraw my arm from her ministrations and brush the lingering sensation from my skin. I already fucked Ama and know she's not my True Mate, but she'd be a good mate nonetheless. The thought sits uneasy in me, though. I blow out a lungful of air. "That's real sweet. But you know I can be a handful."

"I can handle a handful," she says, walking her fingers up my arm.

Abruptly, I stand. "I don't have time for this right now. I've got a vampire problem to deal with."

Ama stands, too, a frown creasing her brow. "Don't get yourself killed."

I hold up two fingers to my chest. "Wolf scout's honor."

I head for the beat-up old pickup, not looking back at what is sure to be disappointment painted all over Ama's face.

Engine roaring, I speed down the wet street, spraying water in a rooster tail behind me. I have a new plan that doesn't include the fucking vamps.

At least not directly.

Once outside the city limits, I floor it and roar toward Wild Wolf Swamp, aptly named, since our clan used to live there.

Now, it's nothing but a waterlogged cesspool where panther shifters hunt and old-timers like Sterlina Vayzen cling to their tiny plots of land and take refuge at Gideon's Bar during floods. I wouldn't be going there at all except that Sterlina's the most powerful diviner in the area, and though I'm convinced I don't have a True Mate, I have to make damn sure before I choose someone else to fill the role. I can't imagine a worse fate than giving up and having a brood of kids with some other woman, only to then find my True Mate.

When I arrive at the witch's treehouse, a giant gator crawls from beneath her tree and waddles toward the water, where it slips silently into the murky, liquid embrace of the swamp. More gators make their presence known by the bulge of their eyes lining the surface of the water. Spanish moss drapes listlessly from the trees as if exhausted from the incessant heat, and vultures line each branch, watching as if hoping I'll turn into their next meal.

I hop down from the truck and stride toward the bell dangling from a tree branch, swatting mosquitos as I go. Grabbing the bell, I shake it back and forth, making it clang so loud that birds scatter from the nearby trees and wheel into the sky overhead.

"Think I don't know you're here already, shifter?" calls a voice like dried grass.

Shielding my eyes with my palm, I tip my head back to try and find her, but the sun prevents me from seeing anything but harsh light. "My truck's hard to miss."

"It's your scent that makes itself known, wolfie. That and your intention. You projected your desire to come and see me the second you stepped from your porch." A phlegmy cough rattles her throat. "You're not going to like the answer to your question."

I still can't see her. It's like asking the sun to give me information. "What's the answer? Tell me, and I'll be on my way."

"Not so fast. I need cash."

"How much?" My eyes sting from the sun's assault, but I don't look away. I've heard this lady's tough, but I'm a match for anyone in the area.

She names her price, and I curse under my breath. "I'll give you half that. It's all I've got."

"Full price."

"I don't have it."

"Then I don't have an answer for you. Go on then. Be off with you!."

Nearby, birds chitter and rustle in the foliage surrounding her treehouse.

I squint into the shadows of the thick copse of trees flanking her dwelling. "Come down so I can talk to you face to face," I say. "I like to see who's swindling me."

"If you don't have the cash, we have nothing to discuss," she says. Her words sound like leaves rustling in the wind.

I dig into my pocket and retrieve a fat roll of cash. It's supposed to hold me until the end of the month. "I can give you two-thirds of what you asked."

"Nine-tenths," she counters.

"I won't be able to eat human food for two weeks," I say. My ears fill with silence. If I give her two-thirds of what I have, I can live on whatever we bring in from the hunt. Not ideal, but I've done it before.

A rope with a mesh bag slides down from her tree-top deck.

I count of most of my cash, place it in the bag and yank on the rope. "It's all in there."

"Good. If it isn't, you just lost a lot of money."

Sweat trickles down my neck and soaks my sleeveless shirt, and I swat more mosquitos as I wait. Above me, I hear a faint, steady swish of paper on paper as she slowly counts the bills. "All right, wolf boy, here's your answer."

"Are you sure you know my question?" Another round of silence greets me. I hope I haven't pissed her off enough to make her go back on our agreement after she nabbed my cash.

Several gators slide beneath the swamp surface, leaving a rippling wake where eyes once watched me.

"You have a True Mate."

My chest constricts, and excitement races through me. All those years of holding out weren't for nothing after all.

"Who is she?" I ask. "And where do I find her?"

"She is a wolf named Luna. Look around you, and you will find her."

"Luna?" I scratch my head, trying to remember if I've heard the name mentioned in any meetings with other packs. I know all the Jacksonville wolves, of course, and she's not among them. The only other wolves in the area are the poacher triplets who like to hunt on our territory to piss me off instead of finding unclaimed land to hunt. But that's a different story, and those fuckers are thugs who definitely don't carry a delicate wolf name like Luna.

I try it out in my mind. *Luna.*

It's the perfect wolf name, beautiful and ethereal, like a morning glory or a moth.

And here I am, waxing poetic at just a name. Since having my dick balls deep in Trixie didn't have the same effect, I can safely say she's definitely off the list of potential mates.

Hell, I don't even have to keep a list of potentials anymore. I don't have to pick a suitable mate to help me run the pack, give us heirs, and carry on the bloodline. I have a *True* Mate.

"I don't know a Luna," I admit to the witch. "Can you tell me where to find her?"

The sound of wood scraping wood meets my ears, as if a door has opened. Then, the door slams shut with a loud thwack. I blow out a breath. I know when I've been told to fuck off.

Damn it. I kick a stone as my boots crunch over the stones to my truck.

I have a name. That's it.

Still. Damn. After all this time, I don't have to wonder.

I have a name.

I have a True Mate.

Excitement speeds my pulse as I hop into the cab of the pickup. There could be countless women in the world with that name, but only one of them will be my mate. I won't know for sure until we mate, but I'm counting on having a real good fucking idea before that. They say when you meet your True Mate, the whole world shifts.

But then, they also say you might live next to them your whole life and never know. So, yeah, there's a fuckton of legends and lore around True Mates. Guess I'll know which parts are true when I find her.

I crank up the truck and ease away from Sterlina's domicile, heading home. The windows are down, and the wind rushes in my ears as I speed along the potholed road. I try not to look like a giddy teenager in love. I have a fucking True Mate. The best news I've had since I fought and kept the Alphahood from the last man who dared challenge me—Warrick Armstrong, who was banished from the pack for that stunt.

A True Mate will make me even stronger than choosing a mate on my own. Having a True Mate gives a man respect, as it's rare. I hope she's strong like me, a good fighter, a political strategist.

The only trouble is, I don't know who or where she is. Sterlina said to look around me, and when I asked again, she shut the door in my face. Guess I insulted her by asking what she'd already answered. "Look around you" doesn't mean shit, though. Was I supposed to look around right then, under her treehouse? Is Luna coming to the Jacksonville area soon? Or am I supposed to look for her across the country, across the world?

I'll fucking do it. I have to find her—the sooner the better. The vampires are getting way too fucking cocky.

Ama can help me find her. That's the sort of thing a Second does while I'm running the pack here. Only the last thing Ama wants to do is to find the woman who will fill the role she so desperately longs to fill.

Chapter Two

Luna

Standing knee-deep in murky swamp water, I thrust my bare hands into the catfish hole I discovered a second ago. Some of my wet hair lands in my eyes, making it hard to see. When my fingers curl around the slimy beast, I yank back, lifting my prize high.

"Gotcha!" I crow to the wriggling critter, avoiding its stinging spine. "Dinner is served."

Clutching the fish with both hands, I use my upper arm to push the hair from my eyes. Mama always tells me my light hair reminds her of the swamp buck's hair when it's standing in the sun. Then she always adds, "and your eyes are the color of the sky on a winter afternoon."

Right now, I'm guessing I resemble a drowned fox more than anything.

As I wade out of the water, hauling my bare feet from the mud with each step, a scream pierces the air. I stand stock-still, attentive. The dying fish flapping in my grasp jabs me with its dorsal fin, immediately flooding my hand with an explosion of venom. "You bastard," I say to the fish. I pick the spines from my skin with my teeth.

Another howl lances my eardrums.

"Mercy on the swamp dogs, that's got to be Mama!"

Still clutching the catfish with my now-swollen hand, I take off at a sprint. Nothing can happen to my mother—*nothing*. Mama has been through enough, and on top of that, she's all I've got. After losing Daddy to murder while I was still a pup curled in her belly, Mama broke with the savage pack of demon-dogs nearby and headed for the safety of the swamp. We've been here ever since.

When I was young, Mama took care of me, filling me with the knowledge of every danger in the swamp, the skill to hunt, and the companionship of each other. She taught me that ogres might look scary, but they're harmless to us, since they only eat magic. She taught me how to know when a storm means rain and wind that could take down the little house I built for us six

17

years ago on a hillock in the swamp, so we need to take everything we own and get up in the trees, where the water won't rise.

Most of all, she taught me that danger comes in the form of man, even when they wear the disguise of a panther or wolf. I've never spoken to a soul besides my mother in my life, though when Mama's not looking, I sometimes sneak a wave to the panther shifters in their fishing boats that glide silently through the swamp like gators. If more than one of them's in the boat, sometimes I hear them whisper to each other, "There goes Looney Luna."

That's my name.

I like the sound of it hissing across the water and into the mossy trees, like a secret only the swamp knows.

"I'm coming, Mama," I shout as I sprint through the boggy landscape. If Mama took care of me growing up, that slowly changed after I came of age until now our roles have reversed. I take care of Mama now. So that's what I gotta do right now, when she's shrieking like a panther. Pushing through the underbrush, shoving aside branches, I come face to face with a terrifying sight.

A panther is attacking my mother's human form.

I don't think about it. I pitch the fish into the glade, shift into my wolfskin, and launch my body at the big cat. It drops Mama to fight back. Success! My canine teeth snarl and snap, trying to get purchase on the feline's neck. I manage to sink my teeth into the puma and rip some of the skin from muscle with several mighty shakes of my head.

It's enough. The panther lets out an ear-shattering snarl and turns tail. As it takes off into the swamp, I turn to Mama. Panthers usually leave us alone, both the shifter and regular varieties, though maybe if they're starving, they'll attack. The panther shifters are as wary of us as we are of them, and besides an occasional wave from a fishing boat sliding under the trailing Spanish moss, they've never paid us any mind. They keep their distance and don't bother us, even though technically, Mama says this part of the swamp belongs to them.

I don't have time to think about why that panther attacked. Why doesn't matter, anyway. It happened, and now Mama's in bad shape, and it's my job to make sure she heals. I focus on her moaning form.

"Mama," I say, shifting back to human and crouching next to her. "Mama." Out of the corner of my eye, I spy the catfish still engaged in a listless struggle with death. "Look, Mama. I brought food." I crawl toward the fish, pick it up and bite off the head. Then, like a good wolf pup, I bring my morning catch, gripped in my teeth, to my mother. "Look, Mama, see? Here's food. Eat some and get your strength back."

Eyes closed, Mama sniffs the fish and shakes her head. "I don't need fish, Luna love," she wheezes. "It can't help me. I'm afraid this is it for me." Her voice comes out in a gurgle. Claw marks crisscross her body, and blood seeps from the jagged tears in her skin.

Don't die on me. Please don't die. I'll be all alone out here.

My head whips around as I search for something to staunch the blood oozing from Mama's side. As I search, I swat at the blood-sucking insects attempting to make a meal out of me.

A giant gator drags its body from the slew and makes its way in my direction.

You can smell the blood, can't you, you bastard?

I toss the fish and send it flying. The gator catches it with a snap of its hinged jaw. Then, it makes an ungainly pivot and waddles back toward the water.

I scoop up Mama's limp body with a bit of a struggle and carry her toward our house, the one I built with my own hands when I was twelve years old, according to Mama. I don't know how she knows that.

"I'll get you help," I say as I scramble through the damp bog. "Don't you die on me, Mama!"

She doesn't answer, and I'm afraid she's done for. I swallow hard, tears flowing down my cheeks before I offer the suggestion that comes to mind. I only dare speak it in a small voice, and only then because I'm not sure she'll hear. "Maybe the other wolves can help?"

A fierce growl emerges from my mother's throat, and her eyelids pop open, staring at me from a long-ago time and place. "No wolves. Never the wolves. They killed your father. Never trust a wolf!"

"But Mama. I don't know what to do," I say, rounding the bend with a noisy splash through the swamp water. "I don't know how to fix something this bad, and I can't lose you!"

I sniff up my tears and scramble up the bank toward our house, out of breath from carrying her weight.

Mama's breathing comes weak and shallow "You're eighteen," she wheezes. "That's full grown in the human world, and you came of age as a wolf a long time ago. I raised you as best I could. It's time to let me go. Remember all I've told you."

"No!" I cry, kicking in the door to our home. As I enter, I lurch to a halt.

There's someone in our house.

Fear bolts through me like lightning strikes. The intruder is a woman with long, glossy hair the color of the night, like the panthers. Is she another one here to finish us off? What did we do to offend them?

"Are you a wolf known to the panthers as Looney Luna?" she asks.

"Who wants to know?" I say, backing against the tin wall. My arms shake with the effort of holding my mother's body, so I squat and gently lay Mama down. Then, I move in front of her to protect her.

The panther-haired woman shakes her head and gives me a look I can't decipher. "I'm Ama, and I came to fetch you. Our Alpha has requested your presence."

My head whips around to gaze at my mother. If Mama didn't bark out a retort, it means she's unconscious… Or *dead*. I reach out and shake Mama's still form. "Mama. Mama. Are you with me?"

Mama lets out a low moan, indicating life still thrums through her veins. But she doesn't speak.

"Didn't you hear me?" the Ama-woman says, speaking in Mama's hurry-up tone.

"Of course I heard you," I snap. "I'm not deaf."

"Then let's go." Ama stands tall and steps toward the door, and something in her commanding presence makes me want to quake. But I stand firm, for Mama.

"I'm not going anywhere. *You're* the one who should leave."

I cross the packed-earth floor in two steps and reach for one of the plastic water jugs I use to catch rainwater. I pour water into my favorite cup, a tall, red plastic glass that you can see through when you hold it up to the light, that I found floating in the swamp one day after a flood. Maybe it'll let the light shine from Mama again, too. I turn and make haste back to her side. Crouching, I lift her head with one hand and try to get her to drink some water with the other. "Come on, Mama. Just a little water."

The water simply drips onto her face and pours off her chin.

"She needs more than water," Ama says, crossing her arms and raising her chin.

"Are you a healer?" I ask hopefully. She hasn't attacked yet, so that's a good sign, but I don't know her, and Mama told me to never trust strangers. Everyone's a stranger, so I don't trust anyone.

"No," says Ama.

"Then you should probably shut up." I use my index finger to pry open Mama's lips, then pour a little water into her mouth.

A violent coughing attack ensues.

"Shit, shit," I say, setting the glass of water to the side. I help Mama to sit up and whack her on the back a few times, desperation making me cry again. "I'm sorry, Mama. I don't know what to do. Tell me what to do!"

Mama collapses in my arms as her blood pools on the dirt floor.

"Damn it." I press my fists to my stinging eyes, my mind reeling. I know how to deal with Mama's moods, her quiet spells, her thinking things are out to get us. I know how to bandage scrapes and put poultices on bruises and swellings and snake bites. But this... There's too much blood.

"I can help you," the Ama woman says.

I lift my tearstained face. "What can you do? Are you a shaman? A witch?"

"No," Ama says, tipping her head to the side, but not like she's curious. She doesn't look interested or sad or scared Mama will die. Her expression isn't anything. "But I know a healer. She can help your mother."

"Why would you do that for me?" I ask, my eyes narrowing with suspicion. "Are you a panther? One of yours just did this to us, so why are you offering to help?"

She huffs out a breath. "I'm a wolf."

My back stiffens and my heart races. This is what Mama warned me about all my life, the moment I've been taught to avoid since I could speak. "Wolves lie," I whisper. "And murder their own kind."

A flicker of something—surprise? confusion?—flashes across Ama's face like a summer storm. "I'm here because you have something my Alpha wants," she says, going back to her non-expression. "And that's why I'm offering to help."

"What do I have?" I ask, giving a panicked glance at the four walls, the leaky tin roof, and the bed of rags.

Ama stabs her finger at me. "You."

"Me?"

She rolls her eyes up and then back down. "Yes, you."

"Then you're shit out of luck," I say. "I can't go anywhere with a wolf. Mama says so."

"Suit yourself," Ama says. "But from the looks of things, your mom won't be saying anything for much longer."

Desperation claws its way to the surface of my heart. I want to be a good wolf pup and obey my mama, but I also don't want her to die. It's my job to protect her. I'm the caretaker now, and I have to take care of her the way she did when I was young. So, I make a split-second decision.

Swallowing hard, I nod at the she-wolf. "Then save her. I'll come with you and see what this Alpha person wants. But then I'm taking her home. Deal?"

"I'd like nothing better, but I'm afraid it's not up to me," Ama says with a sigh.

I don't want to go without a deal, but nothing in my life has prepared me for this. Cuts and scrapes, even broken toes, are healed by our wolves, but serious injuries like Mama's are another matter entirely. And dealing with other people, well, that's even further from my experience than injuries.

But what choice do I have? I need to save Mama, the way she's always saved me. If Ama's lying, and this is a trap, I won't be surprised, but the wolves can't do anything worse than what's already been done. Mama is dying. If I go to the wolves, even if it's against her orders, at least I'll know I did everything I could. If I don't do anything, she'll surely die.

So I make the decision to help her, even if that means doing the very thing she always warned me against, even if it means walking straight into the enemy's lair.

Chapter Three

Luna

The second we emerge from the safety of the bayou, my instincts soar into high alert. Instead of being surrounded by pine-oak and tupelo trees and picking my way through the inkberry or Joe-Pye weed, I find myself on a road, which I've only seen from a distance. Up close, they're bleached-out, hard surfaces with the texture of a dried alligator carcass.

Cars zoom past at alarming speeds. When trekking through the swamp, I'd heard the distant sounds of these beasts and seen them from afar, but up close, the rectangular metal boxes are bigger than a swamp monster and even more intimidating. I stop and shake my head, unwilling to take a step into this foreign land and be trampled by one of their metal monstrosities.

"Oh, for fuck's sake," Ama mutters. "Has Axel made a mistake or what?"

"What do you mean?" I ask, grabbing her sleeve.

"I didn't say a thing," Ama says. She steps onto the hard surface of the road, yanking on my wrist.

I plant my feet and turn to look behind me.

We dropped Mama off at a healer's hut not far from here, and now Ama is taking me to her Alpha. I know what that is from Mama. It's the head of all the wolves, the most dangerous and fearsome of them all. I long for her comfort and wisdom as I take this giant step, but I'm on my own, with only Ama, who seems none too friendly.

Though I wanted to stay by Mama's side until she was looked after by the healer, the wizened old woman with skin the color of clay and eyes like an eagle shooed us away, saying, "Your mother is standing at the edge of a precipice. I must tend to her at once to keep her from jumping."

She assured me it would take a while and that I had better leave while she did her best to save my mother. So here I am. I turn to look over my shoulder in the direction of the healer's home. My voice trembles as I speak. "I should stay here and wait for Mama... Make sure she's okay."

"No, what you should do is get to Axel's so we can burst his bubble and get this over with. Then, when he's accepted his fate is just a fancy that isn't compatible with reality, I can assume my rightful place by his side."

"What does that mean?" I ask again, completely lost by this talk of bubbles and fate and rightful places.

Ama tugs at my arm. "Forget it. Let's go. We need to get you cleaned up, so you look less like a bog hag and more like what Axel wants to see. Although..." Her mouth turns up at the corners in a secretive smile.

I don't like that smile. I pull my skinny frame as tall as I can, though I'm still no taller than her. "I'm not a bog hag," I say loudly. "I'm a lone wolf, and I'm proud of my heritage."

"You shouldn't be," Ama says. "Lone wolves are fools."

I step onto the coarse surface of the road. "What is this stuff?" I ask, crouching to run my fingertips across the textured surface. It feels hot, the way rocks heat in the midday sun. I always thought it was stone, but it doesn't feel like any stones I ever felt.

A loud, blaring sound fills the air, startling me. I look up to see one of the beastly cars rocketing in my direction. Mama told me people ride in them, but this one is roaring like an animal.

I leap out of the road, my heart pounding, just as it whooshes by so fast it makes its own wind—a stinky wind I've smelled in the swamp from time to time when the wind blew just right.

"Christ, you're stupid," Ama snaps. "You almost got yourself killed. Quick reflexes, though." She looks me over the way Mama did last time she was thinking about going to town to get me clothes, a look like she hadn't really seen me in a while.

Ama grabs my wrist in a fierce grip. "This," she says, sweeping her free arm before her, "is a road, also known as a street. It's made of concrete or asphalt. And those things are cars. You never get in front of one when they're moving. Got it? And that, over there…" She points to a group of structures. "That's the shopping mall where we're going to get you cleaned up and buy you some new clothes. No way can I take you to Axel looking like that."

I look down at my nearly naked body, covered with dirt and mud from the swamp and a few old rags of the same color. Before we left, I wound a few rags and Spanish moss around my hips and breasts, the way Mama had taught me to do. "What's wrong with the way I look?"

"You're dirty, smelly, and you look like a wild thing. Axel expects something a bit more… *Civilized.*" Ama sneers, towing me along.

I frown. "Why does this Axel man care what I look like?"

"You'll see." Ama drags me away from the road and heads for the buildings. They're massive and look way more sound than the little house I built. I wonder how they got their stones cut into such precise shapes. I could have built a stronger house with rocks like that.

Ama gestures toward the buildings marked by a sign that says, *Paradise Acres.* Around it, a few cars sit unmoving in the places that aren't marred by long cracks and gaping holes in the ground, which is covered with the same stuff as the road.

"What happened here?" I ask, pointing to one of the holes filled with dirty water. "And why are some of these houses falling to the ground?" I gesture toward a pile of wood and metal a ways off through the weeds.

"They're not houses. They're stores. And shit happened. While you've been shacking up in oblivion in the swamp, the rest of the world has been dealing with the effects of the natural disasters. Winds, rain, hurricanes, storms… You name it."

"That stuff happens in the swamp, too," I say, feeling defensive at her nasty tone.

She snorts. "And I'm sure your little hovel has been knocked down at time or two. Some people have simply given up on repairing something that'll only be destroyed again and gotten the hell out of dodge. Others have built more substantive buildings that can withstand the storms." She points toward a formidable building that looks like it was made of the same stuff as the streets. The words *Lew's Bossy Beauties* are painted onto the concrete.

"Why do you need all these buildings if you don't live in them?"

"You're literally dumber than a rock," Ama says. "We choose to live in the real world. The real world has stores."

"I've never been to a store," I say, feeling a little tendril of excitement growing inside me.

"Shocking," Ama says. "Seeing as how you're basically a bog hag who knows nothing except how to wrestle alligators and catch fish. Now stop asking so many questions. You're making my head hurt."

Despite her nastiness, I let the first smile I've felt all day form on my face. Things are bad, but that doesn't mean there's not good in the world. Mama never let me come to town, even when she went to get supplies every few seasons. She said it wasn't safe. But I don't feel scared today. The cars are a little intimidating, but they seem to follow predictable patterns when I watch them on the road, and I think I can escape them if I stay out of their way, like Ama said.

I'm too busy marveling at all the newness around me to be very scared. Ama swings open the door of the concrete structure, and we enter. Inside the store, a tall, midnight-skinned man grins at us. He reminds me of the panthers that move through the swamps under the cover of night.

"Friends," he says, holding out his arms. "Is this the woman you told me about, Ama? The one we'll be grooming for the Alpha?"

Colorful clothes surround us, hanging from metal tubes, while light streams from glass balls in the ceiling.

My mind swims with all these new sights to take in Half of me longs to head back to the swamp and huddle in our cozy tin house, and the other half wants to touch everything, see if the yellow dresses feel like sunshine and the blue like sky.

The male saunters toward us. I sidle backward, away from him, baring my teeth. I've never spoken to a man before, but Mama told me they are to be feared. This one inches closer and seizes my chin, turning my face from side to side. "Exquisite. Beautiful cheekbones. I think we can do a lot with her."

I snap my teeth at his hand, but he yanks his arm back before my teeth connect. I wrench my face away, glowering at him and trying to back away. Ama gives me a little shove forward, back in his direction. "Don't touch me," I warn, fisting my hands, ready to return to my wolfskin if he tries to attack.

Ama snorts. "See what I mean? I'm telling you, Axel got swindled by that old diviner. This must be some sort of joke because this chick can't be anyone's mate. She probably couldn't find her way around a dick if you drew her a map."

"She does seem a bit... Untamed." The male strokes his chin with his thumb and forefinger, appearing thoughtful. "Mademoiselle, forgive me."

He extends his hand to me. I stare at it. I don't know who Mademoiselle is, or why he's holding out a hand like he'll help me up when I'm standing right in front of him.

Ama chuckles. "He's making a gesture of friendship, dumbass. Take his hand and shake it."

My brow furrows. "Why?"

Ama huffs out a sigh, wraps her fingers around the man's hand, and gives it a small shake. "Lewis, I'm pleased to make your acquaintance. I'm Ama." She turns toward me, her lips pressed together in a flat line. "That's how we greet people outside the swamp. Think you can manage that?"

I try it, taking Lewis's warm hand and moving it up and down. I've never touched a male before, but his hand feels the same as mine or Mama's, only softer. It feels warm and nice enveloping mine, but I pull away quickly. Mama said not to trust people outside our family.

"Say what I said, but use your name instead of mine," Ama says to me before meeting Lewis's gaze. "I have to spell out the most ridiculous things to her. I thought I was getting his mate, not babysitting an overgrown toddler."

"She seems a bit feral," Lewis says, gazing at me with soft eyes. "But she's not so bad."

We exchange names the way Ama did. "I'm Luna," I say when it's my turn. "You don't seem so bad, either."

Lewis throws back his head and lets out a deep, coyote-like laugh. "That's wonderful. I think I'm going to like you, Luna."

Then, he turns away from me and extends his hand again, only more from his side than straight on.

"What do I do this time?" I ask.

"You take it—but only if you're willing—and we proceed to my cave of mysteries." A smile spreads across his face and up into his dark, sparkling eyes.

Behind him, Ama glowers.

I went in a cave with Mama once, and it wasn't scary. I avoid Lewis's hand but follow him when he gestures toward a back room. Hardly the kind of shelter I expected, I'm confronted with a room where pieces of fabric in various colors are draped over chairs scattered around the area and a huge mirror. A table in front of the mirror is covered with tiny pots of color and sticks with soft-looking furry ends. I reach out a fingertip and stroke the end of one of the sticks.

"She probably doesn't know what that is," Ama says with a sneer.

Lewis picks up one of the stick-things and explains, "This is a makeup brush. And this is a hairbrush. We're going to use it on your abundant tresses once you've taken a shower." He waves a piece of wood with boar bristles poking out of it.

"A shower? Like rain?" I ask, dizzy from all the new information.

"Sort of."

I pick up a jar with blackish goo inside from a rack next to the table. "What's this?"

"This is hair dye," Lewis says, grabbing the jar and replacing it on the rack. "Some people like to use it to turn their hair different colors. We'll not be doing that to you today."

"Why not?" I ask, wondering what different colors of hair I could have. I never much thought about my hair because I never knew I could change it. Looking around at all the colors of fabric in the room, I think of all the colors in the world that my hair could be. Blood red, or sunset orange, or pink as my tongue; blue as twilight or green as a coiled fern.

Ama scoffs. "Let's not make ourselves more of a freak than we already are."

Lewis grabs my shoulders, pivots me around, and marches me toward the corner. He urges me inside an outhouse-sized room with golden-green walls like dragonfly wings that smells damp, like the bog. Only this dampness smells sweet, like springtime flowers. Metal things protrude from the wall. Lewis twists one of them, and water pours from another metal device on the ceiling. "Strip out of these rags and step under the water. You can use any of those bottles…" He points to several items on the floor. "And wash your hair and your body *thoroughly*. Got it?"

I nod, wondering how to use the bottles. Of course Mama and I washed ourselves. Sometimes we stood in the rain, especially in summer when it was hot out and the rain chased off the bugs for a few minutes. In winter, we collected rainwater and heated it over the fire to have a warm bath, standing outside and rubbing ourselves with a wet rag that we dipped into the water to rinse. I decide this isn't so different, except the rain comes from the wall and the bottles must be used to squirt more water on myself.

"We'll be right here. Holler when you're done." Lewis nods and backs away, shutting the door behind him.

I'd like to go check on Mama, but there are no windows to escape. Since I'm curious about the shower, I peel off the moss and rags and step under the falling water. A gasp of pleasure escapes my lips. It's warm, and it covers my whole body at once instead of just a bit dribbling from a rag while I stand outside, hurrying to clean myself before I freeze my buns off. This… This is *wow*.

Dirty water streams down my body, heading toward holes in a metal grate on the floor. I pick up a bottle, but it's not empty, so I can't fill it with water. I open it, and the smell of flowers comes out. I tip it up and pour some of the contents into my hand, using it to wash my hair and body *thoroughly*, as Lewis instructed.

When finished, I twist the metal thing, and the water stops. Soaking wet and feeling amazed, I open the door.

Lewis's jaw drops when he sees me. He grabs a thick sheet of fabric and hurries toward me. "Let's get you a towel, honey. Here you go. Dry yourself off and put on this robe."

He seizes a white, fluffy garment from a hook on the wall and hands it to me. After drying myself and donning the robe, I let Lewis comb out my tangled hair and do something called "styling" to it. After that, he brushes various powders and creams onto my face and dresses me in some silken garment that feels wonderful against my skin. Finally he stands back and looks me over.

"You look fantastic. Doesn't she look amazing?" He turns to Ama, who looks up with a scowl.

She sits in the corner in one of the wooden chairs with a small rectangular device that she's been tapping with her thumbs every few minutes since we met. "Sure. You always do good work," she says to Lewis. She shoves her hand in her pocket and passes him some green papers. "Will that be enough?"

"This is more than enough," he says, clasping his hands beneath his chin. "Tell your Alpha thank you from the bottom of my heart. He's as generous as he is handsome."

Ama laughs. "Don't encourage that man's ego."

I stare at myself in the mirror. I've been dressed in a waterlily green top and pants the color of cattails. The garments feel smooth and supple, and they don't restrict my movement, which I like. My face has no mud or dirt, only a powdery substance Lewis brushed on my skin, black goo on my eyelashes, and pink cream on my lips.

I look so different from the girl I know from looking into pools in the swamp. I'm not sure who I look like, but it's not me. And I feel as odd as I look.

"Let's go, chica," Ama says, seizing my wrist once more. She drags me out of Lewis's cave of mysteries, through the big room with clothes, and out the door into the bright sunshine.

I want to slug her for dragging me around like the catch of the day, but she's stronger than me, and my wolf instinctually obeys the commands of an older, more intimidating wolf.

"Where are we going now?" I ask, blinking into the glare of the afternoon sun.

Ama lets out a sigh of irritation. "We're going to meet Axel, our Alpha. He's your True Mate."

Chapter Four

Axel

Ever since Sterlina the Seer told me who my True Mate would be, I've had dozens of fantasies about the kind of woman I'll meet. I picture wild and stunning, svelte and shadowy, gorgeous yet strong. What I haven't anticipated is this wisp of a barely adult woman who stares at me from my front porch with all the ferocity of a puppy.

Jesus Fucking Christ. Is it even legal to breed her? She looks like a mere child.

I study her through my screen door. Even with all the make-up, as well as the curve-hugging clothes, she looks like jailbait. Sure, she's pretty, but I prefer real women. Still, it doesn't really matter. She's my True Mate, and if she were only eight, I'd just have to wait for ten years to be with her. Sometimes that happens, though it's definitely not ideal, especially in this situation, when I need an equal at my side to help lead the pack.

But this is what I've got to work with, so I put on a presentable smile, ignoring the snide expression my Second has on her face and hoping Luna is older and less timid than she looks. It could be an asset if she's fierce as fuck but looks unimposing.

That hope is dashed when I let my wolf surface for a second, and she drops her gaze so fast he barely has a chance to see her, let alone show dominance. Opening the screen door, I welcome them both, standing over them with a simple Alpha command. "Come in."

Luna drops into a half-crouch, like she's going to shift and tear my throat out. "What kind of hex did he just lay on me?" she hisses over to Ama. Even her voice sounds young.

"It's not a curse. Axel's making you feel welcome." Ama gives my mate a little shove toward me. I flash my Second a glower. Her disdain for my True Mate is evident, and she needs to remember her place.

In a blur, Luna whips around, shifts into a wolf, and pins Ama to the porch floorboards. Just as quickly, Ama shifts and rolls to pin Luna, and for a second, I think this game will be over with one dead wolf, and it's obvious who will win.

It's not an option. Though we haven't formed the True Mate bond, that comes before even my Second.

"Enough!" I growl, and both werewolves still.

That's a good sign. Luna recognizes my stature as an Alpha, even though she hasn't been bonded with the pack, which means she's submissive. And she might be diminutive, but she's tough... Although I'm not sure what kind of person just shifts in broad daylight and attacks another person with no provocation.

The females shift back to human. Both of them now sport a few scrapes, but they're intact for the most part. They're also naked, their clothes lying in tatters on the floorboards. I've seen all my wolves without clothes before and after hunts, so nudity is hardly notable, but damn... Maybe it's because she's my True Mate, but seeing Luna for the first time makes my cock jerk inside my jeans like I'm the damn teenager. But I don't have time to admire my new mate because there's always another fucking fire to put out around here.

The shewolves scramble to their feet, eying one another warily.

"I said *enough,*" I grit out.

Ama bows her head, but Luna stares at me defiantly. I have to force myself to keep her gaze instead of staring at her sexy little tits. They're so fucking perky.

I stare her down, and she drops her gaze and ducks her head, a submissive wolf instinct that has nothing to do to with her feelings about me. Though she's not a member of the pack, and therefore can't be compelled, any wolf can sense dominance and defer accordingly.

Her manners leave something to be desired, but that will come soon enough, when she's integrated into the Jacksonville pack and learns our ways. All the more reason to bring her into the safety of the pack as soon as possible. Tonight, I'll introduce her as my True Mate, and she'll begin to learn how we operate.

I hold the door for her, and she grabs up her clothes and skulks past me while Ama remains on the front porch.

"Ama," I say to my Second, a warning in my voice. "I trust you found my True Mate easily enough?"

She needs to remember who she's dealing with. Luna isn't just some stray pup we're absorbing into the pack. She's going to be the Alpha's mate, which is a tricky position filled with endless, delicate intricacies if said mate is less dominant than the Alpha's Second. One look at Luna shows she's as submissive as they come.

"Easily as expected, given the terrain," Ama says, a touch of frost to her voice. She jerks on her clothes as she speaks, tying her shirt in front where it tore when she shifted. "It took a bit of asking around, but once I enlisted the help of a couple panthers to find exactly where their place was, I found her soon enough." She gives me a haughty look, and I know she's proud of her sleuthing and that I should be, too. But the attitude she's sending my way is close to crossing a line.

"Thank you," I say grudgingly. "We'll talk later."

She bristles at not being invited in, included in what to her must seem like pack business. But I want a chance to meet my True Mate, to marvel at her existence. This afternoon, while I dealt with a puffed-up teen wolf who thinks he's going to challenge me in a few years, Ama found Luna. Once she located her, she checked in with me, letting me know the condition she'd found her in, but I know nothing about her. I'd like to know her personally for a few minutes before she becomes the latest pack business.

Ama grits her teeth. "Will that be all, sir?"

"It's been a long day for you," I say, trying to appease her with my concern. "Go home and rest up. Pack meeting tonight."

She stares at the porch's rotting wood, a frown on her face. I know I should replace the boards, but with all the shit I deal with on a daily basis, I hardly have time to keep my own house fixed up. It will only be torn apart by the next storm, anyway.

"As you wish," Ama mutters at last, resentment boiling in her voice, like it's my fault the True Mate mark didn't show up on her arm when I fucked her. Without another word, she pivots and strides away.

I sigh and close the door, turning to take in my True Mate for the first time without a distraction or audience. She stands stiffly in the center of my living room, her breath chuffing quick and shallow in her lungs.

"So," I say, striding toward her. "Here we are." She's pulled her clothes on, arranging the shirt to cover her tits and not much else. Her midriff is bare and almost emaciated, her hipbones jutting out above the top of her pants. Lone wolves are seldom healthy and well-fed, so I'm not surprised. A few months with the pack, and she'll fill out and look more like a woman capable of carrying my child than a mere girl.

I circle her slowly, taking in her scent. The perfume Ama applied to her can't mask her natural odor. She smells earthy and delicious, and suddenly, her age doesn't seem as big an obstacle. If I thought fucking someone was the only indication of a True Mate, now that I'm meeting mine, I know it's so much more than that. I'm instantly, unnaturally drawn to her, so attracted to her that I feel my cock stiffen from her scent alone.

I find myself hoping she finds my scent equally appealing, something I never worry about with others. As I circle her, she pivots, eying my every move.

She's got fire, I'll give her that, but it's fueled by suspicion, if her attitude is any indication. Once she's adjusted to our ways, she'll be a lovely addition to the pack, and though she's younger than expected, in time she'll grow to be a match for me, tempering my dominance with her submissive nature and cooling my impulses with diplomacy and tact, something that both Ama and I lack. Submissive wolves are highly valued, maybe more so than dominant ones, since they can calm the storms that so often brew between hotheaded alpha types. I hope she'll be a skilled political strategist in no time, not only helping relations within the pack but between our pack and other supernaturals.

I come to a stop in front of her and tip her chin up with my forefinger. She tenses but doesn't back away. "What are you going to do to me?" she asks.

"I've been told you're my True Mate," I answer. "Once we confirm that, you'll have one of the most important roles in the pack. I'm the Alpha, which means together we'll rule our pack and maintain order in our territory." I tip her head side to side, noting the natural beauty lurking behind the makeup. "How old are you?"

"Eighteen." The word comes out in a whisper. Her luminous green gaze stays fixated on mine. "You?"

"Thirty," I say, releasing my grip on her chin. At least she's not as young as she looks. We can be mated right away and begin soothing relations with the vampires. I became Alpha when I was her age, and if I could run the pack on my own at that age, she can certainly learn the ropes at my side.

She backs away. "What do you need me to do before I go home? I already told that Ama woman that I can't stay."

I can't help but laugh. She's not just naïve to the pack's customs. She doesn't seem to know the most basic laws. "If the True Mate mark appears as predicted, you'll be staying here," I say, offering her a reassuring smile. "It's dangerous for lone wolves out there, especially young ones, and most of all for young, unmated females. You'll be safe with the pack."

Ama told me she lived in a shack that looked like it could barely withstand a windstorm, let alone a hurricane. My house isn't exactly the Knight brothers' mansion, but it's comfortable, and now that I have a reason to fix it up, to make it the home my mate wants, I'll bust my ass to do just that.

Instead of excitement, I see only trepidation in Luna's eyes.

"That's not what my mama taught me," she says, shaking her head slowly. "She says wolves can't be trusted. I might be murdered like my daddy before me. You'd best save us both any trouble by letting me go home right now."

As we looked for Luna in the weeks after my visit to Sterlina, I'd asked old man Waters about wolves who might have left the pack before I became Alpha, and he mentioned a murder and the disappearance of the man's wife. In itself, death isn't any more rare among werewolves than it is humans. We live rough lives, have hot tempers, and can turn into vicious animals at the drop of a hat. What's rare is a woman choosing to leave the pack bond and set out as a lone wolf instead of grieving with the pack.

But once the pack bond is severed, a lone wolf is just that—alone. She chose to cut ties with the pack, and they respected her decision. No one knew she was carrying a child… Until now.

"We can discuss this later," I say to Luna at last. "Tonight, I'd like to introduce you to the pack."

Her eyes go wide, and she crosses her arms over her chest, her lip jutting out in defiance. "I don't want to."

"Why wouldn't you want to meet the pack?" I ask, confused.

"They're not my pack," she says, her chin rising. "Mama and me are lone wolves. We don't need a pack. We got each other."

"Okay," I say. "I understand that's how you lived up until now. But that way of life leads to this—your mother's in critical condition, and you have no one to protect you. That's what the pack is for. They'll protect you."

"She said you'd say that."

"She did?"

"She said wolves are liars and tricksters, and you'll tell me what I want to hear. And here you are. I don't know you, and I'm not about to believe you!" She turns and bolts toward the back of the house.

In a few quick strides, I catch up to her, my arms wrapping around her. "Where do you think you're going?"

"Home," she says, and her voice quavers. "I don't like it here, and I don't like *you*."

Her words slice through my anger. This is not the kind of happy introduction I anticipated. How can anyone not care that they have a *True Mate*? It's like walking away after finding out you won the fucking lottery—and that the ticket is held by the love of your life.

"You'll feel differently once you're bonded with me and the pack."

"No, I won't," she hollers, kicking to free herself. "I will never be bonded to anyone but my mama. Never never never!"

That's about enough of her tantrum for me. I pick her up and throw her over my shoulder, amazed at how light she is. She's just a whisp of a girl, but she's also eighteen, which is way too old for this shit. "You're just going to have to learn to accept it," I growl, stalking out the door.

I carry her down the front steps and toward my truck. She shrieks like a banshee the entire way. No doubt the neighbors are getting an eyeful of my new mate and me, if they're not already at the cookout, preparing for the meeting.

I place Luna on the passenger seat and flatten a hand against her torso, pinning her there. I stare her down, my wolf rising to the surface to show his dominance. "Stay," I grit out.

She stiffens but drops her gaze, her submissive nature unable to stand up to mine for long. I rarely use my dominance against a submissive—I rarely have to. Submissive wolves usually don't challenge dominant ones this way. It's something I've had to do with other dominant wolves more than I'd like lately, though. I thought taking a mate would fix that problem, but if she's the mate, I'm not so sure. I expected a woman, not a headstrong little brat.

I crush the urge to bend her over the seat and fuck her hard and deep, forcing her submission until she's bonded with me and has no choice but to bend to my will. But that's only fun when the woman is being a brat on purpose because she wants that treatment. So I slam the door in Luna's face and circle the truck, grinding my teeth in irritation and frustration. It's one thing to be new to a pack and not know our customs, but Luna's doesn't seem to understand how to be a werewolf at all.

I hate to admit it, but I'm relieved to be joining the pack for dinner, so I don't have to deal with the crazy on my own for the rest of the night. Luna is… A lot. I thought I was getting a partner to help me, not a child to raise. She turns to the window, crossing her arms and sulking as we zoom along at an ungodly speed like the devil's on our tail. We sail past boarded-up buildings, decrepit, decaying parts of town, and head for the place we all gather—the Creebay Preserve at the edge of town.

All the wolves in Jacksonville hunt in the Creebay Preserve, though we all live in town, most of the pack making homes in the same neighborhood as mine. The preserve is our hunting ground, and though we could get there in a few minutes of brisk running, I don't trust Luna not to take off.

The preserve is seventy-five acres of old-growth oaks, magnolia, and water oaks, with creeks and saltwater marshes throughout. It's teeming with life, and it belongs to our pack. I'm hoping Luna will feel at home here, too. As I drive, I calm my temper and try to see things from her point of view. She must be rattled at her departure from the swamp into the God-awful city Jacksonville has become after decades of storms.

When we arrive at the picnic area, the scent of cooking meat tickles my nose and stimulates my growing hunger. I park the truck at the edge of the clearing, hop down, and circle the hood to open Luna's door. Before assisting her down from the truck, I hiss in her ear, "Behave."

"Why should I?" she snarls. "You don't listen to what I want."

"Just behave," I repeat. "You're here to meet the pack. They're not enemies, Luna. They're here to protect and welcome you as my mate. They'll be your new family."

"I don't need a new family," Luna says, her lip quivering. "I've got Mama."

"And now you'll have so much more," I assure her, taking her hand in a firm but gentle grip and leading her away from the truck.

Members of the pack have already started a fire in the fire pit. A deer is roasting on a spit over the flames. Several wolves lift their hands in greeting as we approach.

"Greetings, Alpha," Hati calls to me from across the fire pit.

"Jacksonville pack," I say with a nod. "I've got someone I want you to meet."

Luna yanks her hand away from me with a low snarl.

I whirl to face her. "That is not behaving," I growl in a deadly voice. "You are going to meet my pack—*your* pack. If you give them a chance, they'll welcome you with warmth and hospitality. Can you stop with the suspicion and give them the benefit of the doubt?"

She glares at me, extends her hand, and stiffens. I take her hand and lead her across the sandy clearing. Everyone is waiting, watching my new mate, a wolf they've never met. No one even knew she existed, since we don't hunt in panther territory, where her mother retreated after leaving the pack eighteen years ago.

The rest of the pack—Adolfa, Lobo, Borris, Bleddyn, Chann, Trixie, and the others—form a half-circle.

"Jacksonville Pack," I announce in a loud, clear voice. "Meet my True Mate, Luna."

I draw her hand toward my lips, intending to kiss her knuckles. When I feel her resistance, I flash her a warning glare.

She relents, but I doubt the effect looks exceptionally loving. When I glance at my packmates, some give me sympathetic smiles, some appear confused, a few shake their heads.

As I release my grip on her hand, my anger starts to boil. It's not like I'm asking to mate with her in front of them. The girl could chill the fuck out a little.

Adolfa, sweetheart that she is, comes to my rescue. Hurrying over to Luna, she smiles warmly and extends a hand. "Welcome, little one. You're downright lovely. We're all mighty pleased to make your acquaintance.

Luna smiles uncertainly and shies toward me. My chest swells with warmth.

"I'm Adolfa and those squealing monsters over there—" With her free hand, my packmate points to a group of children splashing in the saltmarsh through the trees. "Are my kids. Well, at least a few of them."

Luna shakes Adolfa's hand with solemn precision. "I'm pleased to make your acquaintance."

I turn and smile broadly at my pack. "My Luna is tired from her journey. She's had a long day. Let's all make her feel welcome."

"Of course," Lobo says, stepping forward. He, too, extends his hand to Luna and introduces himself and adds, "I'm Adolfa's mate."

Luna repeats her overly formal greeting, introducing herself to him.

Then, in turn, each pack member does the same. I stand by proudly, watching my mate meet her new packmates. When they've finished, Luna looks a bit overwhelmed, so I wrap an arm around her waist to comfort her. Instead of relaxing into me, she tenses.

"Let her have some breathing room," Adolpha says, prying Luna from my grip. "I'm sure our new member would like some girl talk after a day with you."

I growl low in my throat at the thought of being separated from my mate, but Luna's grateful smile at the older female lets me know she welcomes the idea. With a grumble, I relent and go attend to some business with Hati. After all, if Luna is to be my True Mate, she'll have to learn to be left on her own at times.

When I reach Hati, I glance back at Luna, who eyes me from a couple of yards away. I smile at her, and she pivots away, quickly following Adolpha. But she was looking, watching me. Does she already feel the attachment the way I do?

"Do you have all the needed weapons for our siege?" I say in a low voice to Hati.

Standing much shorter than my six-foot-six height, Hati draws himself tall and leans in. "Sure do, boss. Lobo and I forged wooden bullets. Enough to put the motherfuckers into the afterlife ten times over."

"Good," I say, frowning and squeezing the back of my neck to ease some of the tension from my muscles. "Then we're set for the night of the full moon."

"A month from now, we'll be rid of the bastards." He pauses and nods over to where Luna and some of the women are talking. "She's the one, huh?"

"According to Starlina," I confirm.

"You went to see that old witch?" Hati says with a shudder. "She scares the shit out of me."

"She's formidable," I admit. "But I needed information, and she's the one who could give it. That little sprout over there is apparently not just my mate, but my True Mate." Smiling, I turn my head to gaze at Luna only to find her in a half-crouch, pivoting in a circle of females. Same as on the porch, she looks like she's about to wolf out and launch into an attack.

"Stay back," she hisses, holding out a hand in front of her as if to ward them off.

"Jesus Christ," I mutter, rushing to retrieve her.

"Ladies," I say, nodding as I take Luna's arm and drag her away from the others.

"Let me go," she shrieks, wrenching her arm free and drawing the attention of some of the other wolves in the pack.

"What the fuck?" I growl.

"Th-they were getting too close," she says, looking a bit chastised. "I was scared."

Her big blue eyes blink up at me, her expression so lost that I want to comfort her.

"Guess I shouldn't have left you to fend for yourself," I say, my irritation melting. "Just stick with me through the rest of the evening."

She nods mutely, allowing me to put a protective arm around her as I lead her back to the others. Second thoughts creep in. Could Starlina have been fucking with me? She could be wrong, or it could be a different woman named Luna. The pull I feel for this pup could be just pity and my own dumb hope that somewhere I'd find a True Mate. More likely, I don't have one at all, like most wolves, and I should take a mate in whoever is most able to help me lead the pack.

It was a mistake to bring Luna before the pack so soon. I should have mated her first to make sure. My Second appears, sauntering from the woods, and my thoughts turn to her. Is she the one fucking with me? Is this her sick way of making a point, that just because someone is labeled a True Mate, that doesn't make them a good match or able to lead. Ama has what it takes. If shewolves were Alphas, she'd be one. She'd certainly be an excellent choice to stand beside me against encroaching supernaturals—she's cunning and strong and fierce.

Everything the waifish girl beside me most certainly is not.

I glare at Ama but gesture for her to join us. She better hope she's not playing a prank on me because there's not one thing funny about this shit.

"Yeah, boss?" she says, once she's standing in front of me. Her face is neutral, void of expression.

"I want you by my side through this event," I order.

Her eyes flit to Luna, and a flicker of scorn crosses her pretty face. "More babysitting, sir?"

A growl rumbles in my throat, but I don't push my dominance at her. I want her compliance out of respect, not because I force it. "Do as your Alpha asks."

"Understood," she grits out. She follows me to the picnic tables, and she, Luna, and I sit. Adolpha hurries to place the first plate before me while her mate serves Luna and Ama. Then they go to fetch their own plates.

Luna looks excited for the first time today, a feral smile on her face as she eyes the deer and roasted vegetables. She lowers her head, grabs the meat between her teeth, starts gnawing like a dog with a bone. She hunches over her food, snarling and growling I reach over, ready to teach her some fucking manners. What the fuck? She grew up with a lone wolf, but this… This is beyond that. She's like an animal even in human form.

Everyone stares with pitying looks on their faces or avoids eye contact when I glare at them. Beside me, Luna continues eating like a savage, meat juices dripping off her chin. Is she doing this to piss me off? Or does she just have so little shame she doesn't mind completely humiliating herself in front of my entire pack? Fury builds inside me as I watch her scoop up a handful of vegetables with her bare hand and shovel them into her mouth.

This *feral child* can't possibly be my mate. I wanted someone who knows what she's doing, someone clever and powerful, an equal to me. I need someone to help me run the pack and hold back the encroaching vamps, not an infant without basic table manners.

Only Ama meets my eyes, a challenge in her gaze as if she's silently saying *I told you so.* "You could always dissolve the bond and take someone of your choosing," she reminds me.

My stomach hardens into a stone. "I didn't know this is what Luna would be like," I admit. "But I'm not doing that."

"Suit yourself," Ama says with a shrug, spearing a carrot on her fork and popping it into her mouth with an arched brow, her eyes cutting to Luna, who's picking her teeth with a fingernail.

I'm so pissed I don't even know who to direct my anger at— Ama for being a smug bitch, Luna for being a complete imbecile, or fate herself for cursing me with this mate, if that's what she is. I find myself hoping this is a joke, that someone is fucking with me. Right now, it seems preferable to having a True Mate who doesn't understand basic human decency.

We finish the meal in tense silence. Plenty of wolves are rough around the edges, and our manners probably leave something to be desired if we were dining in high society, but Luna is something else. She snatches more meat several times and eats like a wild dog, getting food on her face and hands and wiping it on her clothes. When it's time to go, I'm beyond fucking ready, but Luna has other ideas and tries to take off into the woods. The whole shitty ordeal ends with me throwing her over my shoulder and carrying her kicking and screaming back to my truck.

And if I thought things couldn't get worse, I'm going to have to mate with this creature to secure our bond and get proof that we're True Mates.

Chapter Five

Axel

In the truck, I roll down the windows, letting the hot, damp air in. Luna pokes a finger out into the air rushing by, then sneaks a glance at me. When I don't reprimand her, she sticks a hand out, spreading her fingers and letting the wind stream between them. A shy smile spreads across her face, growing bigger as she hangs her arm out, swooping it up and down through the air currents. I offer her a smile, and she laughs, turning back to the window. She's like a little kid playing airplane with her hand.

Maybe I was too hard on her at the picnic. I should have eased her in more slowly, gotten to know her before I showed her off to the pack. I'll just have to teach her a few things before I take her out in public again. I can't have the pack thinking my mate is some kind of idiot.

By the time we get home, we've both calmed down.

"Where's Mama?" she asks, peering off into the late evening darkness.

"She's still at the healers," I say. "I'm sure she'll come right here when your mother wakes up. So this is the best place for you to stay until we hear back."

Luna looks hesitant, then nods. "If she's going to bring news here, I'll stay."

"We need to confirm that we're True Mates, anyway," I say. "Are you ready to do that?"

She nods. "I'm ready."

I'm a little surprised she's so willing, but it only makes my life easier, so I lead her inside and up to my bedroom. The room is sparsely furnished—just a king-sized bed, a dresser, two nightstands, and a closet—but it's big enough for the two of us to cohabitate nicely. While Luna washes up, I close the curtains to give us privacy and light some of the candles I had Ama buy for the occasion. Now that we're alone, I'm more relaxed. If she's a defiant animal in front of the pack, it makes me look weak. If she's an animal in the bedroom, I won't even try to tame her.

Luna emerges from the bathroom and perches on the edge of the bed, gripping her hands together in front of her. "What do you need me to do?"

"We're going to mate," I say, coming to sit next to her with enough space between us, so she doesn't feel crowded. "That's how the True Mate bond forms. Once we have the mark, we'll know for sure that we're made for each other."

She nods, swallowing hard. "Where do we do this... This mating?"

I pat my bed. "Right here."

Her lungs rise and fall in a sigh. "What should I do?"

I'm not surprised she's a virgin, but I'm a bit surprised by how pleased my wolf is at the knowledge that she hasn't mated before. I usually like a woman who knows what she's doing, but Luna isn't any woman. She's my mate, and knowing that she'll only ever be mine makes my wolf swell with pride. She was made for us and us alone, and we will take what is ours and give her all the pleasure she's never had in return.

"All you have to do is lay back and enjoy it," I say. "It hurts for a minute the first time, but then it feels good." My cock begins to stiffen at the thought. I've heard stories about how amazing it is to fuck a True Mate, like nothing else on earth. We have plenty of time to learn each other, for her to learn what she's doing and for me to learn her body and how to give it pleasure. It can only get better from here.

"Mama told me about True Mates," Luna says. "I thought it was something you were, not something you did."

"It's both," I say. "Once you go into heat, I'll breed you, and you'll produce an heir to raise. Hopefully many heirs. Our leadership will be even stronger with many pups."

"Where do I find them? Do I have to search the swamps and saltmarshes?" Her brow furrows into a quizzical expression.

"No, my love," I say, taking her hand. "You'll give birth to them. They'll grow inside you."

She gazes down at her stomach, sweeping her head slowly from side to side. When she lifts her head to gaze at me, her blue eyes stare at me in confusion. "Like I came from Mama's belly?"

"Exactly like that," I say.

"So an heir is a baby?"

"Right," I say. "*Our* baby."

"Well, I don't go into heat no more," she says. "I did once, but I wanted to leave the swamp, and Mama said we couldn't have that. So she got a spell put on me to suppress it from then on."

"When was that?" I ask.

"I don't know," she says. "A long time back. I think I built the house around then."

I nod. "We'll get that spell reversed. An Alpha must breed his mate and give her heirs."

My cock throbs at the thought of breeding her, filling her with my seed and my children. My wolf growls at me to take her and claim her now, to breed her full of our babies. But I know she hasn't been seeking a True Mate like we have, and she deserves tenderness and care her first time, to I push back my wolf instinct and focus on my mate.

"How about a nice shower to relax?" My cock engorges even more at the thought of holding her in my arms beneath warm water.

"That's when it rains from the ceiling?"

"Yes," I say with a nod. "Would you like to do that?"

"Can I scrub all this shit from my face?" She taps her cheek.

"Yes, you can scrub all the shit from your face. I'll even help."

Her luscious lips part, and she nods shyly. "Okay."

This time she doesn't resist, taking my hand when I offer and letting me lead her to the ensuite bathroom. The walls are covered with black and white checkered subway tiles. The sink is slightly stained with rust from the pipes, and the white-tiled shower is small, but there's room enough for two.

I lean into the shower stall and turn on the hot water. When I turn around, Luna has already stripped, and I suck in a breath at the sight of her stunning, petite little body. This time, I don't have to keep it professional in front of Ama. I take my time, drinking in the sight of her perky little tits, the nipples a soft, rose-petal pink that makes me want to lick them. Her belly is flat, but I have a feeling that before a meal, it will be concave—until I fill it with my heir. Her ribs protrude more than they should, and her hips aren't yet wide enough for childbirth, no doubt delayed in growth by malnutrition. I intend to fix that first thing, feeding her until she's plump before her next heat, when it's time for her to grow round with child.

When my eyes dip lower, to the tangle of pubic hair covering her mound, my mouth waters and my erection cries for release.

"What?" she asks, her voice an octave higher, a mixture of defensiveness and uncertainty.

"You're so fucking beautiful," I say, scanning down her long, coltish legs, which are too thin but nicely muscled anyway. I imagine them wrapped around my waist as I send her into throes of ecstasy. Waiting for her to get skittish, I take a slow step forward, giving her time to protest. When she doesn't, I lift a hand, then hesitate.

"Can I touch you?"

She nods mutely, and I cup her breast, gently stroking my thumb over her nipple. It's so soft I can hardly feel it against my calloused skin, as if I've brushed wind instead of skin. Her lips part in a gasp, and my cock throbs harder, precum leaking from the tip already.

"You can get in the shower," I say, stepping back to shed my clothes and toss them to the side.

"What's that?" she says, pointing to my cock.

"This is my cock," I say, running a hand down my thick shaft, teasing her a bit. I cup my swollen balls in one hand. "And this is where my seed is. I'll put my cock inside you to mate, and it spills my seed into your womb."

Again, I wait for skittishness, but instead, she wrinkles her nose as if it's distasteful and picks her way past me. She steps into the shower, tips her head back, and closes her eyes.

Gorgeous. I clench and unclench my fingers, my wolf panting and eager to explore her naked body. I ease into the shower behind her.

Her head jerks up, and her muscles grow taut. "What are you doing in here?"

"Easy, love. I'm going to help wash you." I squirt a dollop of the shampoo sitting on the ledge of the tiny, frosted window into my hand and proceed to massage her wet hair. "You're doing great."

She closes her eyes and lets her shoulders fall away from her ears. It's progress. I'll take it.

"You smell amazing to me," I murmur as I lovingly rub my fingertips against her scalp. My rigid cock nudges her bare ass as I work, but she doesn't protest.

She presses her palms on the tiled wall in front of her and lets her head fall back, which causes her perky little tits to rise.

Saliva fills my mouth. Damn, how I long to suck those perfect rosebud nipples, make her tremble and whimper for more.

I turn her, and the water streams over her closed eyes and face. Streaks of colorful make-up infused water stream down her body and are carried away in the drain beneath her feet. Gently, I run my fingers over her cheeks and her neck. And then I can't help myself—I lower my mouth to her neck. I nibble and suck my way down to her collarbone, murmuring her praises, stroking her wet nipples with my thumbs again until they stand as erect as my penis.

She tenses for a second, then relaxes, as if consumed by sensation.

"When we're mated, we'll form the True Mate bond, and we'll be bound together for life. I'll protect you always," I breathe into the shell of her ear. "And your mother."

A sweet smile forms on her lips, and I know I've said the right thing. She gazes up at me, hope dawning on her face. "Always?"

"Always, my mate," I say, matching her smile with mine. "Trust me, and I'll make you feel good."

She sways closer, and I pinch her nipples gently, then slide my hands down her slippery sides to her narrow hips. Crouching, I take one of her hard nipples into my mouth, sucking gently.

She lets out a little moan.

"Does that feel good?" I say, easing back.

"Yes," she says through a gasp. "So good."

"You taste so good." I massage both breasts while I suck first one rosy nipple and then the other. My cock is about to explode with need, but I beat down my wolf and force myself to be a patient man. I've never wanted someone so badly, so ravenously. My wolf roars for me to consume her, to fuck her raw and hard, to dominate her until she breaks and then put her back together again with so much love and care that it shatters her all over again.

She is *mine*. Ours. And my wolf sure as fuck wants to claim her as such.

Instead, I hold myself back, kneeling in front of her like the goddess she is.

"What are you doing?" she asks, peering down at me with curiosity and suspicion.

"Now I'm going to taste all of you," I say, my voice husky with desire. I push her gently back against the wall and spread her delicate lips to reveal the pink bud of her clit. My cock throbs more precum, but I ignore it, leaning in and inhaling her scent. Her smell is divine, like nectar to my soul. Overcome, I let my mouth descend on her untouched, virgin flesh, lapping at her pearly clit and tasting the glistening pink slit of her cunt.

She lets out a whimper, her thighs quivering as the tip of my tongue finds her tiny opening and prods it, tasting inside. I've eaten plenty of pussy, but none have tasted like hers, like the sweetest dessert waiting for me to gorge myself like a glutton. I force my tongue into her virgin entrance, and she cries out in pleasure, gripping my head with both hands. I grab her legs and throw them over my shoulders, burying my face in her, sucking and licking and thrusting my tongue into her until her juices drip down my chin. Her cries echo through the bathroom as she comes, gripping my head and riding my face hard with no inhibition.

I can't wait another minute to be inside her tight little pussy. I reach behind her, turn off the water, and stand.

"Was that it?" she asks, looking dazed with lust. "Mating?"

"That was just the beginning," I say with a cocky grin. I dry her off with a soft towel and scoop her up, carrying her to the bedroom like a princess. I throw the covers off the bed and lay her down gently, standing over my tiny bride ready to be ravished by my wolf and my cock.

"Lie back," I command, spreading her knees and gazing down at her slick pink cunt. Her clit is swollen and a deeper pink now, her delicate folds glistening with readiness. She does as she's told, panting with eagerness, her eyes dazed by what just happened. My own head spins with a desire like nothing I've ever known, a hunger as insatiable as a vampire's as I inhale deeply of her perfect scent, made just for me.

"You're a masterpiece," I murmur.

Reaching down, I stretch her opening wide with one hand and work a finger into her tiny hole with the other. She gasps, tensing up. The clench of her walls around my finger makes my cock threaten to erupt cum all over her like a geyser.

I force myself to focus on her, sliding my finger deeper until I feel the barrier of her virginity. I long to thrust my finger through, but that honor belongs to my engorged cock. I lower myself between her legs, taking my cock in my hand and stroking the swollen head up and down her slick folds.

"This will hurt at first, but try to relax, and the pleasure is even more than what I just gave you."

Her eyes close, and she settles her head onto the pillow. She reaches up, her tiny hands gripping my broad shoulders. "I want more," she moans.

"That's it, Luna love. Just let me pleasure you. You have no idea how happy I am that I've found you." I practically purr as my heart floods with joy at having discovered my True Mate, the one made just for me and my wolf. My wolf roars with lust and joy inside me, frantic to take what's ours. She raises her narrow hips, and I look down at her perfect little body, reminded again how small and fragile she is beneath my powerful body. All the more reason to treasure her and treat her like the precious creature she is. *Our mate.*

I rock my hips against hers, coating my cock with her fragrant juices as her knees open and she arches up, seeking our completion. I can feel her wolf calling to mine, the way mine is to hers. They want to be one, to join, to make the unbreakable bond that only True Mates can share.

I lower my mouth to hers and kiss her gently and thoroughly, holding myself back. As she responds to my kiss and finds her rhythm with mine, I fit the head of my erection to her tight, virgin entrance and press. Nothing happens for a moment, and I have to apply more force than I expected to breach her opening. When her flesh yields and my bare tip breaches the vicelike grip of her unopened pussy, her fingertips dig into my biceps and she cries out, the sound echoing into my very soul.

"It hurts," she gasps.

I ease away from the kiss and bring my mouth to her ear. "It will only hurt for a bit," I whisper. "Relax and I'll make love to you until all you remember is pleasure."

She nods, blinking a tiny teardrop from the corner of her eye. I wipe it away with my thumb, overcome by a swell of love and a primal need to possess my mate that can't be stopped. With a groan, I force my cock deeper, opening her channel for the first time until I feel the barrier of her virginity stretch and then slowly tear around the head of my cock. She cries out again, and I bury my thick length all the way inside her tight little pussy, claiming every inch of her sacred depths for my own.

Her walls clamp down around me so tight I think I'll erupt inside her instantly. I hold myself back, forcing myself not to fuck her hard and raw, pounding her into the bed until she screams my name. I can feel the head of my bare cock pressed up against her cervix, and all I want to do is breed her, seed her belly with my babies right here and now.

"You are *mine,*" I growl, my wolf surfacing. She nods, biting her lips together, tears pooling in her eyes. I kiss her gently, but my wolf will not be held back any longer. He wants to release our seed deep inside her. A roar tears from my lips, and I drive into her tight flesh again and again, feeling a bond forming with each powerful, claiming thrust. She cries out each time, but she doesn't fight destiny. She spreads her knees wide and gives herself over to me completely, her tiny little body absorbing the brute force of my thrusts, submitting to my need to possess her delicate little body and wild soul. An overpowering sense of love and ownership and completeness fill my chest, a raw joy I never imagined possible.

She is my True Mate.

She is *ours.*

Apparently you don't have to cum to know. I can feel it in my blood, my bones, my wolf, my *soul*. I feel a burning ache at the base of my cock, and realize I'm starting to form a knot, something I thought was only legend, something that happens only with a True Mate. A shocking heat throbs in my arm, like a brand is searing into my skin.

Luna shrieks, grabbing her own arm. A glowing white crescent moon appears on her skin, branded by the power of the ritual, of our bond, of the rightness of our union.

I want to roar my pleasure and come and come and come, spurting my potent seed inside her until she's overflowing. But I know that once the knot forms fully, she'll have to come too before we can be separated, so I hold back, waiting for her.

"What's happening?" she cries. "What are you doing to me?" She shoves me away, her eyes full of panic that tells me neither of us will be coming.

Fighting back my wolf instinct to finish the claiming and breed her, I roll to the side. My erection, still pulsing and slick with her blood, slides from her wet core. "It's the True Mate bond forming, Luna. This is a good thing. It means we're bound together forever. I'll love and protect you for eternity." I reach to comfort her, but she jumps from the bed, her eyes wild as she reaches between her legs and pulls her hand away bloody.

"I don't want eternity," she screams. "Why do I feel this way? Did you cast a spell over me? Make it go away!" She digs at the glowing mark with her fingernails, drawing blood from her arm, too.

"Luna, no," I protest in horror. "What are you doing?" I make a grab from her, but she ducks aside and races from the room.

Fuck!

I've found my True Mate only to be rejected by her before we even finished mating.

Chapter Six

Luna

The glowing moon on my arm burns as I race through Axel's house, and my core throbs with raw pain and unfilled need, like he put an empty spot inside me that only he can fill, and it will always be empty now, always crave him returning to fill it. Blood trickles down my legs along with my own wetness, but I ignore it and the call of my mate as I run for the door. It seems I've been branded, something mama once told me people called "cowboys" do to their cattle. When they're branded, the cowboy always knows which cows are his. I didn't know they had to mate them first.

Does that make me Axel's? Now that he's mated me and branded me, do I belong to him instead of myself and Mama and the swamp?

I hear his footsteps behind me, like he's coming to claim his property the way Mama and me claimed our little hillock in panther territory and chased off anyone who tried to crowd in. The house was big enough for only two, and the hillock only big enough for one house. But my body is not Axel's house, even if he was inside me. My body is my house, and there's only room for one.

I run outside, scent the air real quick and then take to my wolfskin. It's easy, since I'm not wearing a stitch of clothes. I run fast, racing back toward the woods and the swamps where I belong. This whole crazy day feels like a bad dream, the kind I had when I was a kid where I'd wake up shrieking like a panther because I was sure I was drowning, that the swamp had come alive and was sucking me under the mud and muck, where I couldn't breathe the way an ogre could.

This day is going to drown me. There's too much of it, too many things that happened too fast, without giving me a chance to breathe or think them over. There was the attack on Mama, and the Ama wolf, and the pack, and Axel.

Axel.

A little ripple goes through me, making my fur stand on end as I run. He scares me, and he's so big, big as an ogre, but not as harmless. But my wolf craves him again already, craves his touch and his nearness, his scent, his wolf, his wildness, his possessiveness. My wolf wants all the things my human mind doesn't. I have to force her to keep running away from him, to not circle back and run to his house and slip onto his sheets and let him fill me with so much pleasure I think I'll break apart at the seams, the way the part he called a cock broke me apart between my legs, in the place I call my heat.

That's the part that ached and throbbed and felt so good and so bad at the same time when I went into heat the one time before Mama stopped the torture by giving me potion every time it started to come back. Only when Axel sank his cock deep, deep into the core of that heat did it wake up again. That's when I knew what I'd wanted and needed that time, when I was in heat. I'm not now, but I still want to feel it again, even though it hurt like a knife inside me and made me bleed. I crave him filling the aching need, the emptiness he filled me with even as my soul cleaved to his.

I'm almost through the woods and back to the swamp when a man slides from the trees like a midnight shadow.

His skin matches the dark sky overhead, and there's a faint red glow emanating from his onyx eyes. He must be one of

Axel's packmates, though I don't remember him. I should have smelled him, but maybe I was too busy warring with the thoughts in my brain that are swarming like swamp rats in a flood.

I take a few sniffs, but he *has* no scent except for the faint whiff of ash. How is this possible?

Facing him, I bare my teeth and snarl.

He puts out his palms. "Easy," he says, his voice deep and smooth and accented with a strange tint of something different than anyone I met today. "I mean you no harm. I was just out hunting in the woods. Same as you, little wolfie."

I've never been outside the swamp, but I know this is no werewolf. At least, not one I've met. He doesn't smell familiar at all, and I wonder how I'd know if he was a friend or not. I decide to shift back to human and ask. When I emerge into my human form, I shy back, baring my teeth still. "What are you?" I hiss. "How come you have no scent?"

"I have no idea. How is it you *have* a scent?" He smiles broadly, revealing two of the longest, pointiest canine teether I've ever seen. They're longer and sharper and thinner than wolves' or even panthers' teeth.

I ignore his question and cant my head to the side, studying him. "You're not a wolf?" I ask, making a guess.

"Far from it," he says easily.

"Well, I'm hiding from the wolves. So don't tell them you saw me."

"Good plan," he says. "The wolves can't be trusted."

Instantly, I relax. This man speaks my language—the language Mama spoke. Hearing her words from him assures me that he can be trusted. He's on my side, just like she was.

"They captured me," I say. "But I escaped."

"Is that so?" he asks. "And how long were you with them?"

"Only a day," I answer. "But they want me back. They're chasing me right now, so I'd better go."

"Don't go so soon," he says. "And you can't possibly escape a wolf pack on your own. Maybe I can help."

"Their Alpha thinks I'm his True Mate," I say, showing him the mark on my arm. "But I can't be. I have to find my mama and go home. She's at a healer's at the edge of the swamp where we live, in panther territory."

"You must mean Bogbeast Waters," he says, arching one midnight-black eyebrow.

My eyes narrow as I regard him. He doesn't seem hostile, though, and Mama only told me to watch out for wolves, not other things. Most other creatures don't bother us—the panthers always left us alone until today, even though we claimed a tiny spot in their territory; ogres don't bother with wolves; and catfish only sting because they want to live, same as any other creature.

"You know the place?" I ask. Just then, a howl sounds someway off, and a shiver clutches at my backbone like a cold hand rising from the swamp. My wolf threatens to erupt and drag me back, answering the call. It must be Axel and whatever spell he cast over me that gave me the mark on my arm. I almost choke with the need to go to him.

The tall man snaps his fingers, jerking me back. "Tell you what," he says. "It's late, and it seems you truly are being hunted, so why don't we go somewhere safe? I'll guard you against the wolves tonight and in the morning, I shall take you to the healer's place so you can check on your mother. Did the healer live in a dome-shaped, canvas yurt, painted with red symbols?"

"Yes," I say, relief washing through me. "That's the place."

"I know her well. Her name is Artuna. What do you say? Come and rest a while. In the morning, we'll be off. A young thing such as you shouldn't be out at night with all the predators around. And surely you're too small to be a danger to me, even if you *are* a wolf."

"Do you think I could go home instead?" I ask, my voice small. I'm tired and I just want to rest my head in the familiar, comfortable little house I've always known.

"Oh, I don't think so," he says. "Not tonight. If the wolves kidnapped you, they'll know where to find your house. They'll never think to check my place."

"Okay," I say reluctantly, glancing at the shroud of the swamp's darkness with longing. He's right. Ama was at my house, and she can tell Axel where to find it again.

"Good," the man says. "I'm Evan, by the way."

I wonder if he expects me to repeat the words Lewis taught me, or if I can sniff him and get more information that way. But he doesn't seem to require a handshake, and when I hear footsteps in the distance, I know there's no time for sniffing.

"Come then," Evan says, and before I can say a word, he scoops me up in his arms and shoots through the forest at breakneck speed, even faster than I can run as a wolf. Trees blur by like they did in Axel's truck, and only a moment later, he's stopping in front of a large dwelling near a running creek. I don't see how this can be a place to hide, as the house is huge and made of some kind of white stone. I can barely see the water in the night, but the trickling sound is like a balm to my ears, and the damp scent of moss fills my heart with comfort.

Pushing aside the massive steel door, he sets me inside and says, "Welcome to my lair."

Something about this lair-house makes me uneasy. Despite the hot night outside, the air inside feels chilly and dry and dead. I glance around, hugging my naked self. Timbers crisscross the high ceilings overhead, but everything else in the house feels unnatural and cold, from the shiny, white stone floors to the silver legs to the chairs and glass tables beside the couches.

Suddenly, I miss the wooden house with peeling yellow coloring the outside walls that my mate lives in. It was big and fancy compared to mine, with things inside it that don't have names in my vocabulary. But compared to this, it was small and homey. A shiver crawls up my spine at the thought of living there, with a wolf who is apparently my True Mate. Longing fills my soul at the thought of Axel, but dread sits like a hulking beast alongside the desire.

I turn toward the door, only to see Evan staring at me expectantly.

"Can I offer you something to drink? Water, perhaps?"

"I can just drink from the creek," I offer, gesturing with my thumb. In truth, I want out of this strange, clean house, want to run back into the familiar chaos of the bog.

"Nonsense. That wouldn't be civilized, would it?" Evan tsks and gives me a reproachful look.

I shrug, feeling as uncomfortable as when Axel dragged me in front of his pack and the whole lot of them stared at once. Never in my life had so many eyes been on me, and it set my teeth on edge. Now, just one man makes me feel as unnerved. Having never heard the word "civilized" before today, how should I know if it's civilized to drink water from a stream?

Evan studies me through one eye while stroking his jaw. He seems to be assessing me, sizing me up like I size up a catfish before reaching down into the mud for it. After a beat, he pivots and strides toward a spigot jutting from the wall. He fills a glass jar, steps in my direction, and hands it to me. "Please, sit."

He points to a grand chair that might be a throne for the kings Mama read books about. It's long and made of silver arms and legs and a white mattress in a seated position. It could fit a whole slew of kings. I know of furniture, since I built a table for our house, and shelves for our things, but Mama and I live simply.

Evan lays a black blanket over the spot he wants me to sit, and I sink into the softness. I'm not used to furniture so large and so grand. I'm not even sure of the name for most of it. Mama and I own something much smaller that we found near the spring for a place to sit during the day. Mildew had begun to claim it, but we set it out in the sun for a few days until the smell had lessened. For sleep, we shift into wolves and curl up on the rag rugs we made out of clothing and other scraps we've found in the weeds. The clothes were covering bones, so no sense in letting them go to waste, and sometimes things wash up or we cross them in our hunts. If we sleep in our wolfskins, we're much more alert to danger, so there's no sense in having a bed, though I know of them from the stories in a couple soft books Mama brought home one day.

I take the water from Evan's hand and sniff it. It has an odd, chemical smell that I'm not familiar with.

"Sorry about the slight taint," he says, smiling a bit. "The pipes are rusted. It's only... It's copper. Yes, yes, it's copper."

"Oh," I say, taking a sip. It sure as heck doesn't taste like the water in the swamp, or even the salt water that floods in during storms. Realizing I haven't drunk anything all day, though, I drain the glass, making a face at the bad taste coating my tongue. "I bet the stream tastes better."

Even grins and takes the glass before returning to the spigot. "Here. Let me get you some more. And tell me, why do you need to hide from the other wolves? You are one, after all."

"I told you, they captured me," I say. My chest swells with pride as I recite the words Mama has said so many times. "But I'm a lone wolf. I don't need a pack."

Evan fills the glass and returns, handing it to me. "I certainly can understand that. I myself am most at peace surrounded by water, trees, and sky."

I'm starting to feel *very* relaxed—perhaps the day is catching up to me. I yawn, my eyelids falling as if chained to the floor. With effort, I manage to drag them open.

Evan gives me a sympathetic smile. "You seem tired. Are you tired? I can fix a bed for you."

"No, no," I say, suppressing another yawn. "I can just sleep here."

I fall back into the plush couch. I could get used to this kind of comfort.

"So, tell me more about this pack of wolves who captured you," Evan says. "How many were there?"

"Oh, yes," I murmur, my lids beginning to close again. "There were a lot of them."

"How many is a lot?"

"Enough to fill a dozen picnic tables," I say, blinking to force my eyes open.

"Gosh, that's quite a lot," Evan says. "Do you think they'll hurt me if they find you here?"

"No," I assure him. "Surely not. They only ever mentioned fighting vampires."

"Vampires," he exclaims. "You don't say!"

I nod groggily. "Right. I've heard of those before. But I've never met a vampire. Have you?"

"Oh, no," Evan says. "Wouldn't that be terrifying? I wonder what the wolves have in mind for their attack?" He strokes his temple with his long fingers.

"I don't know," I say, trying to answer him since he's been nice to me, though I just want to sleep. I let my eyes fall closed, but my mouth keeps going. "I only heard a bit about wooden bullets."

"Oh, that sounds awful. Did they say when it would happen?"

"Full moon," I mumble, then sink into the cushion behind my head. I can't stay awake another second, I'm sure.

When two arms wrap me in the black blanket and slide underneath me to heft me into the air, I can barely respond.

"Don't," I think I mutter, but I'm not sure. And when those two arms gently lower me onto a soft bed and tuck warm covers around me, I still can't budge, falling into a sleep as deep as the dead.

Chapter Seven

Luna

I wake to the sound of crashing that shakes the floors. I sit up, blinking in the blinding sunlight that makes my head pound. For a second, I can't remember where I am.

Then a familiar voice booms through the house, bringing the whole overwhelming day before back to me. It must be midday judging by the position of the sun, but I feel as groggy as if I barely slept. I can't remember ever having slept so late. I must be sick. That explains the headache and the oversleeping.

"Give me back my mate," a familiar voice thunders from another room. "Or you'll wish you could die, you bloodthirsty leech!"

A rush of joy floods my heart at the sound of Axel's voice, and the brand on my arm pierces me with fiery heat. But then I remember fleeing his house, hiding from him, the pain and confusion of the mating ritual he performed.

"I'm not keeping her from you," Evan says. "I'm merely offering her rest. She chose to come here and did so of her own volition."

Loud footsteps tromp in my direction. The door to my room flies open, and Axel looms over me, a frightening expression of fury marring his face.

I feel instantly, incredibly safe when surrounded by his arms—and because I know I'm not, it makes that feeling terrifying, as if my free will has fled like I did last night.

"Put me down," I cry.

"Like hell." Keeping a fierce grip on me, Axel throws me over his shoulder and carries me out into the bright sunshine, sliding into his truck and buckling me into the other side before powering on the vehicle and speeding away down the gravel drive through the woods.

"How did you find me?" I ask, staring at him, my heart galloping in my chest.

He says nothing, but pushes his foot down, making the truck leap forward and careen along the road even faster. I'm still not used to going so fast, and it's exhilarating but scary, too. I grip the strap he bound across my chest, trying to catch my breath over the thrill of speed and sound roaring under us like a giant swamp monster.

"Where are you taking me?" I shout over the noise of the engine.

He still says nothing.

Only when he skids to a stop in front of his house and I lurch against the strap does he turn to me. I'm laughing at the sensation of flying, but it quickly dies when I see the blaze of fury in his eyes. "What did you do with the vampire?" he demands.

"What do you mean?" I ask, shrinking back against the door.

"Did you let him suck your blood?"

"N-no," I say. "I didn't know that's what he was. He was nice to me, that's all."

His eyes narrow, his nostrils flaring. "Like I was nice to you last night?"

"What do you mean?"

"Did you let him fuck you?"

"What is *fuck*?" I ask, unsure why he's so angry, but knowing he's dangerous, like Mama always said. He's twice my size at least, and unlike last night, when his size felt protective and powerful and *right* as he loomed over me on his bed, now it's terrifying.

"Tell me exactly what happened," he says, his voice going from hot as the summer sun to colder than seawater in winter.

"What did I do?" I say, scanning my mind for something, anything I might have done.

"You went to the vampires," he says, his voice still cold, but sad, too, like when I had to tell Mama I didn't get anything for dinner and we'd have to sleep hungry again. "Now, tell me what happened from the moment you met that bloodsucker to the moment you left."

I take a breath and haltingly walk him through every moment, every word we spoke. "Then he gave me something to drink," I finish. "I thought it was water, but he asked me questions, and then I couldn't stay awake and I…" I realize I'm blubbering, but the intensity rolling off Axel scares me.

When I stop speaking, Axel just stares at me.

"So, you don't even know if he drank your blood," he says. "You were drugged. You could have said or did things you don't even remember."

"I didn't!"

"You gave away our secrets to a vampire!" His words blast through me like the bite of an alligator. "Do you understand how serious this is?"

I bite my lip and shake my head.

"This is a crime that carries a sentence of death for a werewolf," he says quietly. "Since you didn't know better, I will ask—hell, I'll probably have to fucking *beg*—the pack for clemency. They will spare your life, since you are the True Mate of their Alpha. But you will no longer be allowed to join the pack, as this is the deepest betrayal a wolf can fathom. My packmates will never allow a traitor such as you to join, and I cannot in good conscience be your mate and put all of them in danger for my own selfish desires. I will go to our shaman and have her dissolve the bond."

He reaches out, stroking my hair behind my ear with tenderness that somehow hurts, when combined with the crushing sadness in his eyes. I don't know what "dissolve the bond" means any more than I know what it means to be bonded. But from the ache in his gaze, I know it can't mean good things for me. As I slump back in the seat, I realize it can only mean one thing for my mother, too—without his protection, she's going to die.

*

Loud footsteps sound on the steps of Axel's home, making me jerk from my position in a huddled ball on the front-room floor. I've been hunched in the corner here for an hour or more, ever since Axel brought me home from the vampire's and then went off to deal with a crisis at another pack member's house.

A sense of elation swells in my chest, telling me he's home. The moon symbol throbs on my arm before he even opens the door. But a far worse brand, the accusation of betraying the wolf pack, hurts even more.

Axel enters, along with Ama and an elder as frail as leaves when they've lost their color and begin the process of decay in warm swamp water.

The elder moves slowly, progressing toward me with an unmistakable elegance, like a deer. A large nut-brown satchel rests on her shoulder, swinging slightly as she moves. "Get up, child," she says in a loud, clear voice that doesn't match her wizened features.

I rise obediently as Axel and Ama stand back, eyeing me as the elder approaches.

My limbs begin to tremble. "What are you going to do to me?"

"I'm going to separate your soul from that of your True Mate," the shaman says, setting her bag on the table in front of Axel's sofa.

"I hear it hurts like a bitch," Ama says, sidling closer to Axel and giving me a smug smile.

"Silence," Axel growls through clenched teeth. "Don't make it worse than it is."

Ama drops her gaze to the floor.

Axel's hands are squeezed into fists, but his eyes are soft as he stares at me with a look that says he regrets this more than I regret going to the vampires. I don't know why, don't understand what exactly it means, but the sadness in his eyes tells me that he does.

The elder retrieves a knife and a long, carved stick painted with symbols. Feathers dangle from the end of the carved wood. She retrieves another wooden wand with something like deer hooves affixed to the end. The dried hooves clatter and set my nerves on edge as she rests them on the table. Next, she pulls out two tiny jars of something that glows like the bioluminescence I've seen in the sea sometimes when I've been exploring with my mother.

When she's laid out all her instruments, the shaman says, "Close all the curtains and lock the doors. We must seal the space."

"Ama," Axel snaps, and Ama rushes around the house, covering the windows and slamming the doors, turning a part of the knob that makes a snicking sound.

When Ama's done, the elder turns to her and says, "You stand as a witness, Second. And you…" She points a bony finger at Axel. "Come and stand before your True Mate."

Axel progresses toward me like he's trudging through quicksand toward his death.

When he stands before me, I blurt out, "It doesn't have to be this way. Whatever I did, I didn't know. Maybe the vampire tricked me. Maybe he cast a spell in the water. Maybe he…"

Axel's lips part as if he's going to speak, but then they press close, and he shakes his head. "Please proceed, Elder Amexaryl."

"Axel," I breathe. "Please don't do this." My arms and legs shake hard like the land when a sinkhole is forming. Tears drip from my eyes as I look at him. I don't know what's happening, but I feel weak and helpless, like a dying animal.

He swallows, a funny little lump in his throat moving up and down, and directs his gaze elsewhere. "I have no choice. The needs of the pack outweigh the needs of the one."

He repeats the words like it's a well-used phrase. Even though he's supposed to be the leader, he must be as helpless as I am, because I can feel the pain in his every word, that this is hurting him in ways it doesn't hurt me.

Elder Amexaryl picks up the stick with the feathers. "Hold onto her, and don't let go until I tell you to."

Axel's hands clench mine, and he gazes into my eyes.

We both stare at one another, and though tears only leak from my eyes, I know he's crying inside. I can feel it, through some strange instinct that makes his pain my own.

The elder draws symbols in the air between us.

I begin to sob.

She picks up one of the jars, opens it, and dips her fingertip inside. She flicks the substance from her finger between us, and the symbols light up and twirl slowly in a circle. Then, she picks up the deer hoof stick and shakes it.

The moon on my arm bursts into flames, searing my skin. I try to wrench away from Axel, but his fingers hold on tight. "Axel, no!" I cry. "Please stop."

"It's almost over," he whispers, his voice a hoarse rasp.

I clutch his wrists, clawing at him, writhing as unbearable pain shoots through my body and deeper than that, into my bones, my blood, the vibration of life inside me.

He, too, appears to be in the clutches of agony. His jaw is clenched, and he lets out a tortured groan, like an animal caught in a trap.

"Help," I cry, not sure if I need help for me or for Axel or for both of us.

Ama stands with muscular arms folded, a victorious smile on her face, like this moment is special for her.

Hatred for her boils in my stomach.

The shaman keeps shaking the feet, rattling them together like a rattlesnake, until I want to scream, to tear my hands off if that's the only escape. The moon mark on my arm sears into my soul, wrapping around some deep seed inside me. I feel a ripping sensation in the core of my being, like someone is ripping my spine out of my body. I shriek, and Axel closes his eyes, gasping as if in pain. Elder Amexaryl mutters strange words as she shakes the wretched rattle. The symbols between us whirl faster and faster, making a high-pitched hum that shreds my ear drums. I scream again, trying to rip my hands from Axel, but he's holding onto me so hard I know he's going to leave marks.

The old woman's voice rises in pitch and intensity.

I've never felt anything so excruciating as the pain tearing through my soul.

"Release her, *now!*" the elder cries.

Axel's hands open. I spring away as he staggers backward, falling to his knees, clutching his head.

Ama rushes to soothe him, but he shoves her away. "Get away from me," he shouts.

Hurt crashes through me in waves. I don't understand how something I can't even see can wound me so deeply. If it were a cut, I would bandage it. If it were a crushed limb, I would tear it off with my wolf teeth just to be rid of it. But I can't do anything, can't escape the excruciating, incomprehensible *pain*. I turn and race from the room, sprint down the porch, and shift into wolf form without stopping to undress. I trip when I'm halfway shifted, thudding to the ground and rolling over and over. Then I run, hard and fast, without seeing a thing. I just run. I dash across the shimmering road, and a car screeches to a halt, a horrible sound rising from it and following me behind the next house.

I don't stop. I run for what seems like days but might be only minutes. I speed past the structures where Lewis cleansed and dressed me. Unbearable pain throbs from the place where the moon once marked me, but I don't care. Finally, I find myself at the yurt where the healer lives. I shift back to human form, stand before her yurt, and batter the door with my palms.

The door opens, and Artuna looks at me with one white eye and one blue one. "I'm sorry, my child."

"Where's my mama?" I scream.

"You're too late," she says. "Your mother is dying."

"No!" I cry, pushing past her. I race to the center of the yurt where my mother rests on a fur pelt, barely breathing.

"Luna," she wheezes. "Is that you?"

I kneel before her. "Open your eyes, Mama. Open your eyes, and let's get you out of here."

Mama's head tips back, and she sniffs the air. Her eyelids flutter open. "You've been with the wolves," she whispers. "Never trust the wolves."

And then, as if that took every ounce of strength, her head collapses on the plush fur.

"Wake up!" I plead. "Open your eyes again, Mama. I was taken against my will. They promised to keep you safe and protect you if I did what I was told. Mama, don't go, don't leave me!"

Healer Artuna's firm fingers wrap around my shoulders and urge me to stand.

I whirl to face her. "Do something," I wail. "Bring her back to me! Please, I'll do anything!"

Her eyes well with pity. "I've done all I can, my child. She's lost too much blood. I'm afraid she's gone. You were blessed to say goodbye. You can stay longer if you'd like to send off her soul." Artuna tries to smooth my hair back from my face, but I can't bear even an ounce more devastation that what's already tearing me apart, turning my body inside out.

I wrench away from her, sobbing uncontrollably as I flee from her yurt. Without thought, I sprint through the woods, throwing myself deeper into the familiar shadows of the swamp, searching for a comfort that I will never find again. Not without Mama.

As I draw near to Bogbeast Waters, my bare foot snags on a vine, and I sail through the air and land with a splash in the warm, murky water.

I'm back in the marshes where I was raised, but there's no comfort for me now. Everything I've loved is gone. There's no reason to rise, to get back up, to keep living. There's only pain in this world.

Chapter Eight

Callan

Ethan is my wingman as we hunt swamp rabbits today—he's on one side, I'm on the other. The helpless little bunny has nowhere to go. I lunge and snap, ending his life with one chomp of my canines. When my teeth connect, I shake the soul free from the rabbit. It flies from the prey's body. Dinner is fucking served.

It's a perfect day to hunt as my brother and I slink through the edge of the woods in Creebay Preserve. The temperature is warm enough but not too warm, and a breeze kisses the fur on our bodies, stroking it like a lover's caress.

We stay watchful for Jacksonville pack members—the pack that owns the land and that Axel, the biggest dick on the planet, commands. That bastard would kill us for taking one fucking rabbit. Thinking of Axel makes my hackles stiffen and bristle. I can't stand the guy, and ever since my brother Warrick challenged him for the Alpha position, the feeling is mutual.

As a result of that little scuffle, we were all banished from the pack.

Nah, who am I kidding? That's straight up bullshit.

Warrick broke from the pack as is customary when a challenger loses. Ethan and I were too loyal to let our triplet go it alone while we remained under pack rule. No fucking way. Lone wolves are all but doomed. So, we all broke from the Jacksonville assholes and went our own way. But we didn't go far. We've never lived anywhere else, and risking the wrath of some other pack is a lot less appealing than fucking with Axel.

We live outside pack territory, but we hunt in the territory that he claims as his pack's. We could hunt elsewhere or just go buy a fucking steak at the grocery store. But we like to chase prey here on the regular just to keep the pack on their toes and give a middle finger to their fucking Alpha.

Living on our own isn't bad. Sure, we miss protection of the group. But we've got each other, a revolving carousel of pussy down at the shifter bar, and we're not exactly the kind of men people dare to fuck with. We protect ourselves just fucking fine.

As I pad through the boggy land, soft and cool to my paws, and out toward the swamp, I catch the scent of another werewolf. I yip to the others and trot toward it, even though it's off pack land and therefore not as fun as hunting. We bound along from one hillock to the next, avoiding the water when possible. You never know when a gator is down there just waiting to snap you in half.

At last, the smell of a she-wolf grows stronger, and I spot a tamped-down gap in some reeds. I leap into the reeds and stop when I spot the body. A waif of a young woman is lying in the weeds with her bottom half submerged in murky water. She'll be covered in leeches, but at least a gator hasn't found her. I snuffle around her body and sense life sluggishly trickling through her veins. Immediately, I shift into human form.

Warrick and Ethan, having caught up, do the same.

"What the fuck?" Warrick says as I shove my hands beneath the woman's armpits and tug her out of the saltmarsh.

"She's alive," I say. "If just barely."

"Leave her," Warrick snaps.

"She obviously needs help," I say. "She's a wolf. Maybe she's trying to escape the pack."

"You always do this, brother," he says with annoyance. "You bring back every bird with a broken wing, and we all have to live with their plaintive cries until they die."

"This isn't a bird. She's a human." Having freed her from the marsh, I reach out and push her messy, matted hair away from her face. Her skin is cool to the touch like she's barely hanging onto life.

Ethan tips his head back and sniffs. "She's a wolf, dipshit."

I bat Ethan's head. "I know she's a wolf. Do you think you're the only one with a nose?"

"Cut it out, you two," Warrick grumbles, and we both fall silent.

Warrick may not have bested Axel, but he's powerful, and he's the most dominant of us all. He needs to be someone's Alpha, and since he doesn't have a pack, he leads us.

"I'm surprised she made it this far," Ethan muses. "A cute little female like that…"

A male lone wolf might make it a few years, but a female? She's as much prey as the bunny.

"What, you want to fuck her?" I demand, suddenly protective of the female.

"I might," Ethan says with a shrug. "If she's close enough to legal and dumb enough to let me."

Not that Ethan's afraid of the law. Humans don't govern supernaturals, and without a pack to keep us in line, we live like outlaws. Our bodies are hard from hard work. Our skin is inked all over and scarred from the many fights we've been in over the years. Locals fear us and hate us in equal measure, and the Jacksonville pack's got orders to kill us if we're ever caught in their territory. They've tried, and we've got the battle scars to prove it. But they just can't shake us for good because Axel's all about law and order, and he won't break werewolf law and come attack us outside of his territory no matter how many times we cross him. Man's got principles, whatever those are.

I give Ethan a shove. "Don't fucking touch her."

"Leave her and let's go on home," Warrick says. "Dinner's waiting."

"What?" I ask, twisting around to glare up at him. "We can't just *leave* her. She needs help."

"Who's going to take care of her? *You?*" Warrick sneers at me.

"Why not me?" I demand. Warrick may be out Alpha, but we aren't afraid of him. We're each equally important, even if he's most dominant.

"We could all use a little female company," Ethan says. "Imagine how easy it would be if we didn't have to go down to the bar to find a piece of ass every time our balls get full."

"You mean every night?" I ask with a sour look at our most promiscuous brother.

He grabs his balls. "These bad boys need relief after a hard day's work."

"If she belongs to *them*..." Warrick jabs a thumb over his shoulder. "Those sons of bitches will be crawling all over our place if we take a she-wolf from the pack."

"If she belongs to the J-ville crew, we get to mess with them a little," Ethan says, with a sly grin that shows off one of his missing molars, courtesy of a bar fight with a fae.

"They already want us dead, asshole. You're not banging her even if she is of mating age." I start to slap the back of Ethan's head again, but Warrick snags my hand.

"Enough. Let me consider this," he says, scowling.

Ethan and I wait, silent, as our brother thinks. I might argue and make my case, but in the end, he has the final word. Always.

Which means this is my only chance to persuade his stubborn ass.

"She'll die for sure if we leave her out here," I say. "She's barely alive now. She's probably not from the Jacksonville pack. Look how skinny she is. She must be a runaway, and fuck only knows what she's been through before she collapsed."

"He's right," Ethan says, eyefucking her tender little body like he wants to put his dick in it right here and now. "If she doesn't belong to the pack, they can't miss her. A gift is what this is. And it just fell into our laps. Are we really going to toss it to the gators?"

"Maybe she was looking for the pack, and she almost made it before her strength gave out," I continue. "Now, we have a defenseless little she-wolf on our hands. One of our own kind. Are we really going to leave a fellow lone wolf to die?"

"Or send her into the arms of our enemies?" Ethan asks.

At last, Warrick grunts before turning to leave.

I look at Ethan and smile.

Ethan doesn't need any more pussy. Women love his outlaw charm. They see his tats and they want to ride him like a motorcycle. I'd be lying if I said we didn't have a certain… Reputation around town. Sometime in the last ten or fifteen years, word got around that we're always good for a few multiple orgasms.

I'm not much better, but sometimes I want more than I let on. Sometimes I'd rather one of those women stick around a little longer. But they always head home to the comfort of their stable lives after a wild weekend with us. As I toss the girl's body over my shoulder and start back toward our cabin, I think maybe we're due for one who sticks around a while.

Chapter Nine

Luna

A long, loud groan leaves my lips as I wake. I try to remember where I am, what happened. I'm in a bed that smells... Foreign. I take a few sniffs. The scent is musky and makes my body warm. I turn my head in the other direction and smell something sour like the way the clothes Mama and I found wrapped around the bones smelled before we washed them. It seems to be emanating from the sheets themselves, which feel a little greasy to the touch.

I think back, trying to remember coming here. An assault of pain, both emotional and physical, launches through me instead.

A bond I never wanted in the first place, torn from my soul.

Mama's eyes closing, never to open again.

With a gasp of shock, I sink into the excruciating aches and gaping holes that leave my body open, vulnerable, and bereft.

Why am I still here? Why didn't I die like I wanted?

Footsteps tromp about somewhere in the house. Men growl and laugh. I struggle to an upright position, finding myself in a small room with the door closed. I quickly scan the room. Clothes litter the floor. A small brown, square metal box sits next to the bed. Curious, I reach out my toe and pry open the door. Cool air wafts onto my foot from the blindingly white interior. The chilled air is a welcome change from the stuffy heat surrounding me.

The box is filled with brown bottles and shiny silver cans. I lean over and pick up one of the metal cans. Sometimes Mama and I found cans like this floating down a creek or inlet. The contents were always strange—some sweet, some bitter, but always thirst-quenching. Mama told me humans sometimes put beverages in the water to get chilled in the Florida heat, and they washed away.

I'm thirsty, so I pry open the little metal gizmo on the can the way Mama taught me and take a long swallow.

It's the bitter kind. Blegh.

The door opens, and a male chuckle interrupts my train of thought. I yelp and drop the can. It lands on the floor, and pale, golden bubbly liquid seeps out onto the floor. I shriek and leap from the bed, searching for something to dab up the mess. Mama and I may not have had many things, but what we had we kept neat. I pick up a soiled t-shirt already getting soaked by the liquid and use it to sop up the mess.

The male laughs. "Don't worry about it. Won't be the last time we spill a beer."

"Who are you?" I say, backing into the wall. "Where am I?"

I'm dressed in a large, thick shirt, black with a gold skull emblazoned on the front. The sleeves are folded up several times over, and it falls to my knees.

"We found you in the swamp looking half-dead." Casually leaning against the door jam, he tucks one hand beneath his armpit.

"Why didn't you leave me there?" I ask, my voice accusatory. "I would have died."

"Is that what you were after?" he asks, cocking his head.

"It would have worked, if you hadn't brought me here," I point out, glaring at him.

"True enough," he says. "I been there. Done that." He lifts his hand to scratch the stubble of fur lining his face. He's the most muscular man I've ever seen—not that I've seen many. I've only seen a handful of men in my lifetime, and most of them in the last two days.

Dressed only in shorts, muscles ripple across his bare chest. Three howling wolves are drawn on the left side, directly over the heart. Bold, blocky letters beneath the wolves read, "Our bond is thicker than blood." Black, patterned bands adorn his upper arms. Flowy writing covers his left forearm, and I squint to make out the words. "We must live together as brothers or perish together as fools."

My gaze lifts to his face, framed by shaggy locks, the rich loam's color. His eyes are gold, like autumn leaves. He has the same musky scent as the sheets.

A smile forms on his face as he studies me. "So," he says, not moving from the door. "My name's Callan. What's yours?"

Should I tell him my name? Mama said never to trust a wolf.

"Why do you want to know?" I ask, my eyes narrowing.

"Just making conversation," he says. "If you don't want to tell us your real name, pick something else. I'll call you anything you like."

"Luna," I say. "You can call me Luna."

He doesn't have to know it's my real name.

He steps across the room and crouches before me—not too close to crowd me, though.

"Nice. Like the moon." He gives me an easy smile. "Tell me why you wanted to die."

Tears prick my eyes. "My Mama died."

"Sorry to hear that," he says, reaching out to wipe a tear away with his big, calloused thumb. "Dinner's ready. Why don't you come out and eat with us? Maybe that will help you feel better."

I yank my head away from his touch. A sob bursts from my throat before I can explain.

Callan studies me, a wary expression on his face like he has no clue what to do. He rises to stand, towering over me like a giant. I cower back against the wall.

"I'm, uh, real sorry," he says, lifting his palms. "About your Mama, I mean." He glances toward the door, and I can tell he wants to bolt. "Maybe I'll just leave you be."

"Okay," I whisper, nodding and trying to keep my tears at bay. For some reason, I don't want him to leave. I feel too alone already.

He blinks and takes a step backward. "If you change your mind… Food's ready."

My stomach lets out a loud grumble. *When was the last time I ate?*

A sunshiny expression like clouds parting after a storm covers Callan's face. "See? You need to eat. Food fixes everything." He extends his big hand to me.

I hesitate, torn between hunger and the desire to crawl back in bed and hope I don't wake up.

"I don't bite," he says, his mouth serious but his eyes laughing as he draws an X shape over his chest with his finger. "Unless you beg me to."

My brow crumples into a frown. "Why would anyone beg to get bitten?"

"It's a joke," he says, making an encouraging motion with the hand he's still holding out. "Come on. Let us feed you."

I take his hand and let him pull me up. Then I touch the fur on his cheek. It's bristly but soft, too. I give it a little tug, curious why anyone would have fur on their face.

"What are you doing?" Callan asks.

"Are you human?" I ask. "What creature has fur on its face?"

He lets out a booming laugh. "I do, that's who," he says. "Now we'd better hurry or the food will be gone when we get there."

I want food, so I follow him out of the room, but my body is on alert and ready to bolt if I need to.

The house is big like Axel's—more than one room—but all of this one rests on the ground instead of having stairs. The same brown bottles and silver cans I found in the bedroom are scattered everywhere, empty of their contents. The smell of their contents, heady and somehow *alive,* lingers faintly in the air. Through a doorway, I spot paper cups littering the counter, a slightly fishy, skunky scent wafting from them. Dirty dishes are stacked in the sink. A mattress covered with tangled bedding is shoved against the wall opposite the kitchen. Piles of dirty, sweaty clothes have been pushed aside, creating a path through which to walk.

"Did a hurricane blow through here?" I ask. "Big winds?"

Callan guffaws and pulls me into the kitchen. "Yeah, his name is Ethan."

Two more enormous, hulking males fill the room with their presence.

"Fuck off," says one of them to Callan, but he's grinning. From the comment, I know he must be named Ethan. He sits at a table with more of the bottles pushed together in the center.

The third male stands back, eying me suspiciously. He's got the countenance of Mama when she was angry and might snap and swat me for no reason I could tell. Something about his overwhelming presence reminds me of Axel, though, and makes me drop my eyes and lower my head.

"Luna," Callan says. "Meet my brothers, Ethan and Warrick."

I timidly raise my eyes to theirs and nod a quick acknowledgment.

"He's the nice guy," Ethan says, stabbing his thumb toward Callan. "I'm the sex god."

The big, scary one named Warrick grunts.

Ethan smirks and gestures toward him. "Just do what he says."

I bob my head, grateful he's made it easy, so I don't have to figure that out on my own. I've never met a soul but Mama before the last few days. I wish Axel could have made things that plain for me, so I knew Ama was mean and he was...

I won't think about him.

Despite Ethan's helpful introduction, I still don't trust him or any of them. We all study each other like we're waiting to see who makes the first move. If I thought Callan was big, Warrick is even bigger. They're bigger than the few panthers I saw shift to their human forms before disappearing into the swamp, and even bigger than Axel. The top of my head only reached Axel's armpit, but Warrick's so tall my eyes are level with his bellybutton. Each of their bodies has been painted with color, the way I used to paint myself with mud while Mama washed the clothes when I was younger, before I took over the washing duties.

Ethan has an image of a winged woman on his chest, cradling three wolf pups. Maybe that's his Mama. Warrick has a bleeding heart with a knife through it concealing his chest. Both men sport the same unruly dark hair as their brother, Callan, only Warrick's hair is the shortest, curling around his ears and sticking out in every direction. The fact that he doesn't know about combs, either, makes me like him a little better. I didn't know until a few days ago.

"Why do you paint your bodies like that?" I say, lifting my hand to point at their bare torsos and arms.

"You've never seen tattoos?" Callan says, flexing his arm to make a snake writhe on his bicep.

"Not until…" I bite back the word "yesterday," remembering Mama's constant warning to not reveal too much. "Not much."

Axel, my former True Mate, had tattoos on his body, too. I remember them from when I saw his whole body without clothes, before he made me feel good and then hurt me. A sharp knife of pain stabs my heart as I think of him. I shove it away. He cast me away, breaking the bond he insisted we make the day before.

"These were inked into our skin," Callan explains. "Paint goes away. These last forever. It tickles a little to get it done, but it's worth the pain."

"Let's eat," Warrick says, his voice like thunder grumbling in the sky before a storm.

Callan takes my hand and leads me to the table.

"We caught some rabbits today," Ethan says, standing and putting his arm around me, drawing me away from Callan.

Callan scowls at him.

"But my fine brother, here…" Ethan flaps his hand at Callan. "He took a stab at actually preparing a meal for you."

I wriggle away from his sweaty arm. The windows are open, allowing the damp breeze into the room, but he smells like he hasn't bathed in a while. It's not a bad smell, exactly, but overwhelming coming from a stranger. I don't mind my own smells or even Mama's, but I'm not used to the potency of his sweat scent.

The smell of cooked meat like I had with Axel's pack wafts from a pot in the center of the stove, drawing saliva into my mouth. The men stand awkwardly around the table, staring at me.

"Have a seat," Callan says, clapping his hands together. "Let's eat."

Once seated at the square, wooden table, Callan takes a big silver scoop and ladles some of the fragrant stew into my bowl. Next, he does the same for his brothers. Mama and I rarely cooked, preferring our meat raw. But this mixture of root vegetables and rabbit smells good. I pause, watching to see how they'll eat. The wolf Adolpha told me I was to eat with metal tools, not use my hands.

Ethan, Callan, and Warrick dive into their meals with enthusiasm, picking up metal tools and scooping liquid from their bowls and slurping it down. When he reaches the bottom, Ethan picks up chunks of meat from the bowl with his fingers and pops them in his mouth, chewing noisily.

Suddenly, I'm struck with the enormity of everything that's happened to me in the last few days. I went from a quiet, comfortable life in the swamp with Mama to... Not even knowing how to eat without being scolded. Tears ache behind my eyes when I think of Mama. What I wouldn't give to have her back, to have our life back, to know that I'm not doing every single thing wrong. I look at the strangers around the table, and somehow I feel lonelier than I felt in the swamp, even the last few years when I did most everything on my own. These men aren't companions. They're strangers, and if I know anything about strangers, it's that they intend to hurt me.

Chapter Ten

Luna

The tragic events of the last few days hit me like a sledgehammer. The disaster of the pack gathering, bonding with Axel, fleeing into the woods, meeting a vampire, and telling him "pack secrets," and the subsequent dissolution of the True Mate bond all collide in my head. I sway in my seat across from the three ravenous males who sit noisily inhaling their meals.

Even though I'm starving, I suddenly can't eat. Instead, I stare at the inked pictures of wolves that adorn the men's bodies. "Are y'all *wolves?*"

I spit out the sentence like a poison seed.

Warrick looks up from his food. "You can smell as well as we can."

Ethan smirks, picks up his bowl, and tips it to his lips, sucking the liquid into his mouth. When he's done, he sits the bowl on the table with a *thunk* and gestures to Callan. "Fill 'er up, brother."

Callan frowns but says nothing as he ladles more rabbit stew into Ethan's and Warrick's bowls. "Not hungry?" he asks me, raising a brow and glancing at my bowl.

"Wolves are dangerous," I say, reciting my own mantra, the one I've been told all my life, because it's what Mama believed. "They lie, steal, and murder."

"Some do," Callan says. "Some are outlaws who have no pack."

"Those are the best kind," Ethan says.

I'm sitting with three of the most dangerous looking wolves I've ever seen. They make the pack look like puppies. Eyeing the open window, I push my chair away from the table and start to rise, intending to bolt.

"Going somewhere?" Warrick says.

I want to run out, but I feel his eyes boring into me, and more than that, his will. The wolf inside me cowers at his dominating attention. I feel her shrink inside me, and I lower my head.

Warrick extends his hand, points at my chair, and snaps his fingers. "Sit."

Meekly, I sit. My heart is racing like a scared swamp rabbit in my chest, and my limbs are shaking. What just happened?

"He meant to say 'please,'" Ethan says with a grin. He's missing a tooth behind his canine, and one of his front teeth has a little chip at the corner. His face-fur is thicker than Callan's, and his hair hangs past his shoulders. He's obviously never heard of a comb, either. But looking at his smile calms me and makes my heart beat in a different, erratic way that I don't understand.

"No, I didn't," Warrick says. "I said what I intended."

My gaze drifts toward the open window. It's big enough for me to leap through and run.

"You ain't making her feel safe, brother," Callan says to Warrick, delivering his bowl.

"Not trying to," Warrick says, crunching down on some bones before snatching up the metal tool and scooping up more liquid.

"Come on, Warrick," Callan said, sounding both pleading and exasperated, like when I was a kid and Mama had to coax me to get up and go hunting early in the morning, before it got too hot outside.

Warrick just grunts and goes back to slurping down his food.

Callan gives me a smile that says he doesn't perform that act much, like he's trying on a smile for the first time. "What do you smell when you sniff us?" he asks.

My belly's bound so tight I'm not sure I can scent anything, but I tip back my head and take a few tentative sniffs. "You smell musky and sweaty," I say. "But not *bad*."

Ethan barks out a laugh and pounds the table with his fist, making the dishes and metal tools rattle. "Did you hear that, Warrick? She says we don't smell bad."

My face heats up like I'm sitting in the sun.

"That smell, darlin', is one-hundred-percent purebred werewolf," Ethan says, lifting his arm and sniffing his armpit. "Divine musk to a she-wolf such as yourself."

"Quit it, you man-whore," Callan says, smacking the back of Ethan's head with his palm.

"You're just jealous," Ethan says, punching his shoulder.

I study them, wondering why they're laughing if they're mad enough to hit each other and fight. When Mama got mad and hit me, I never laughed.

Warrick slices his palm in front of his neck, adding a grunt, and Callan and Warrick grow still. Then the scary one turns his eyes to me. "Where are you from? What brought you to the swamp?"

"Until a couple days ago, I lived in the swamp. Now, without my mother, I'm not sure where I live." I fight back the tears threatening to push free.

Ethan whistles. "No one lives in Bogbeast Waters except the panthers."

Unable to speak through the emotion clogging my throat, I nod.

"Have you lived there all your life?" Warrick demands.

Cowering, I nod again. He has the same forceful presence as Axel, but Axel never made me cower before him and answer questions like this. He acted like I was valuable. Inside, my wolf whines piteously at the mention of our mate. I remind her that Axel didn't value us. He didn't want us. He cast us out. And these wolves… They haven't yet.

"Did you have a community out there?" Warrick says. "Are there more wolves in the swamp?"

"No, only Mama," I whisper.

I glance at Callan, who picks a chunk of meat from his bowl. He pops it in his mouth and chews, giving me an encouraging smile with his cheeks full of food.

"Dang," Ethan says. "So, you've never met anyone like us? No wolves? Only humans?"

I shake my head. "No humans or wolves. Just me and Mama, though sometimes I'd see panther shifters fishing or hunting. We saw ogres sometimes, and there's a swamp monster that's pretty scary. And bog hags, but they run if you try to talk to them."

"You talk to the others?" Warrick asks.

I shake my head. "I'd never talked to anyone but Mama and myself until a couple of days ago, when I was summoned."

My stomach lets out another growl.

"Look, she hasn't eaten a thing," Callen says. "Please eat. We'll stop assaulting you with questions."

I look at each man and the tools they're using to consume the stew. I pick up mine, clutching it in my fist, and dip it into my bowl. I lift it to my mouth like they are, but the slippery food slides right off and splatters back into my bowl.

"Never used a spoon, either?" Ethan asks, laughing.

I shake my head.

"Don't worry, you'll fit right in here," Callan says. "Spoons are entirely optional." With a smile, he drops his spoon and picks up his bowl, lifting it to his mouth to slurp from the edge.

That's what I did with Mama on the occasion we ate from bowls. I'm instantly relieved that they know the logical way to eat, and I'm so hungry I don't want to pick up one tiny bite at a time with the spoon instrument. I pick up my bowl and let the food pour into my mouth. I chew, slurp and devour the meat and bones and broth.

Ethan laughs again, only this time it's a wheezing belly laugh. "Would you look at that? She's completely uncivilized."

I pause, setting my bowl down and wiping my mouth on the back of my hand. I'm ready to bolt, but one look from Warrick has me sinking back to the seat, pinned by some force I can't explain. My wolf whines inside me, but it's not exactly fear she's feeling. It's as if I'm being silently forced to obey.

"Don't worry, Luna," Callan says. "We're all uncivilized, too."

"I didn't mean it as an insult," Ethan says to his brother. "It's cute. I like her."

"Of course you do," Callan grumbles.

Ethan turns to me, setting his huge hand on mine. It covers my whole hand like a wolf paw would. "If we have a problem, we take care of it with fists, not words. Don't take anything we say the wrong way, pup, and you'll fit right in."

Chapter Eleven

Ethan

As I edge away from the table, I crack my knuckles with my thumbs, keeping my gaze pinned on Warrick. I goofed around with Luna too much, and now Warrick is pissed. I hope to put off the ass-chewing that's sure to come my way for as long as I can.

"You must be tired, Luna," I say, my gaze flicking back and forth between Luna and my Alpha.

Warrick busies himself with rolling a cigarette, but I know he's tracking my every move.

"You want me to sleep here?" she says, wiping her mouth with her sleeve and setting down her empty bowl.

"Got somewhere better to go?" I ask.

"No. Now that Mama's gone..." Her voice trails off, and she sniffles.

"Head on into the bedroom, and I'll be there in a second," I say, trying to be helpful by clearing the dinner dishes.

Warrick strikes a match against the table and lights his smoke.

Luna stands, coughs at the tobacco, and shuffles out of the room, looking like a lost kitten. And if there's one thing I'm good at it, it's taking care of the kitty.

As I push aside the Java Jolt cups lining the counter, making space for the bowls and spoons, Callan comes up behind me.

"Don't you fucking touch her," he growls.

I elbow him away. "What, you think I'm that much of an asshole?"

"I don't just think it," Callan says. "I know it."

"Fuck you, dickhole."

"No, fuck *you* if you lay a hand on her," Callan says, bowing up like he's going to fight me.

I fucking hate it when he does that, but when I glance at Warrick out of the corner of my eye, he's taking a drag on his cig, skewering me with his piercing gaze.

"I won't touch her," I say, grinding out the words.

"Good," Callan says.

"Good," I say. But the truth is, I'd do Luna in a hot second if she was up for it. But it's more than that. She's so naïve it's just about painful. The lost puppy vibe she's got going on makes me want to do more than fuck her. It makes me want to keep her safe from the hurts that put that guarded look in her eyes so young.

After I clear the table, I consider taking a stab at washing the dishes, then think better of it. If I don't get in there to look after Luna, one of my brothers will do it. I'm not the only dick around here.

I stride from the room, flipping Callan the bird, and head for the bedroom I've given up for Luna. I don't care one bit. I'll sleep on the floor next to Callan and be just fine.

"So," I say, wandering into my room. "Want me to show you where to get cleaned up?"

"What for?" Luna perches on the edge of the bed like she might take flight at any second.

"It's part of the 'going to bed' ritual," I say, standing before her. I rake my eyes up and down her slender body. She sure is a petite little thing.

"Why do we need a going to bed ritual?" she says, her eyebrows stitched together adorably.

Fucking hell. It's going to be hard not to touch her. "I dunno. So we can be all cleaned up and ready for getting up the next day."

Her lips part, and she scrunches up her nose. I stare at her pretty pink lips, trying not to imagine them wrapped around my thick cock.

"If you're a wolf, too, can't you just shift and curl up on a rug?"

"We could, but we don't got rugs," I say, gesturing to the rough wood floor of the house the three of us built after the Jacksonville pack banished us. "So you'll have to try a bed. What do you say?" I flash her my warmest smile—the one that's melted the panties off one too many women.

"Okay," she says, offering me a shy smile that makes my cock twitch again. She follows me into the bathroom, where I turn on the tap, so my brothers won't eavesdrop.

"First, we brush our teeth," I say, seizing my blue and white toothbrush out of the chipped mug on the sink.

"Brush our teeth?" Her expression is one of complete puzzlement.

"Yeah."

She bobs her head in a nod. "Can you show me how?"

Fuck yeah, baby. I can show you how to do lots of things...

I remind myself of something Callan said after I got my tooth punched out by a jealous goblin. Hey, it's not my fault I fucked his wife better than he could. If she'd kept her trap shut, I'd have one more tooth in my head. I swear, women would be more trouble than they're worth if it weren't for the pussy.

"Not all women are meant for fucking," Callan said to me that day. "You gotta learn to be more discerning, brother."

Not all women are meant for fucking, I repeat in my head as my gaze slides down Luna's bare legs peeking out from below the oversized sweatshirt Callan put on her after dragging her home. It just makes me want to grab her up and wrap her in a blanket and keep her warm.

Instead, I grab a toothpaste tube from the medicine cabinet, squeeze some onto the bristles, and then scrub my teeth before offering Luna a big, foamy grin.

She giggles, which softens her features from wary to something so sweet it hurts the roots of my teeth. It almost feels wrong to want to fuck her now.

But the cock wants what it wants. And right now, it's starting to strain against my shorts uncomfortably. I might have to break my promise to Callan and touch her.

"Your turn," I say, thrusting the toothbrush in her direction. "We don't have extra, but you can use mine." I used to keep a stash of toothbrushes around for the women who stayed over, but that shit got expensive. The women who want to ride my dick usually don't stick around long in the morning, anyway. A quick fuck for the road, and they're out of here before their boyfriends or parents can worry about where they've been all night.

I turn on the water and fill my hand with some of it. After slurping it into my mouth, I swirl and spit into the rust and soap-stained basin, then twist the spigot off. When I straighten, my eyes fall on Luna's pretty lips wrapped around the handle of my toothbrush as she studiously and clumsily manhandles the brush against her teeth. A little frown of concentration pulls between her brows, and between that and the thought of my toothbrush, still wet with my spit, inside her mouth, it's all I can do not to back her against the wall and show her a few more things I can do.

"Would you look at that," I say. "You're great at that. Keep on doing what you're doing." I stare at her mouth as a little trickle of saliva escapes and trickles down her chin. I swear my dick is going to shred my shorts at any second. I'm definitely going to need a good tug session tonight.

"I guess I need to learn how to do all this kind of stuff, don't I?" Luna asks.

"If you're going to live here," I say, tugging at my shorts. I'm sure my tip will be peeking out of the hem of my shorts if I don't get the situation adjusted soon.

"I'm not sure about that," she says through a mouthful of toothpaste.

"I'll teach you everything you need to know," I say, cranking up the water. "Here. Scoop, swish, and spit."

She does so, bending over the sink so her ass nearly touches my dick.

I can barely stand the tease. Is she fucking with me? I don't know the first thing about this chick. Maybe she fucked her way halfway across the country to get here. Maybe she saw my raging hard-on and wanted to bounce her skinny little ass on it.

"Thank you," she says, straightening and waving my toothbrush in my face. There's not an ounce of artifice in her innocent expression.

Yup, just me being horn dog.

I take the toothbrush and consider leaving it unrinsed and jerking off with it in my mouth later. Her sweet smile makes me feel like a fucking pervert, though, so I rinse the damn thing in the running water and plunk it back in the cup.

"There," I say. "Ritual complete."

"That's it?" she says, looking up at me with her soft, blue eyes.

"That's it. There's not much to it. Sometimes we take a shower, but the shower head's broken, so…" I shrug.

"That's too bad," she says, lingering in the tiny closet-sized room with me, like she doesn't want to leave, either. "I like showers."

Fuck. I'm sure she's not trying to fuck with me, but that doesn't mean she's not doing a fine job if it by accident.

"Then we'll get it fixed," I say, making a mental note to head to the hardware store and steal a showerhead.

She bites her lower lip, batting her big eyes up at me. "Thank you."

"You're welcome."

The room is way too fucking small for the two of us, and if I don't get out of it, I'm going to do something that will get my ass kicked, so I reach past Luna and push the door open.

"You're ready for bed," I say, my voice gruff.

She nods and steps out of the bathroom. I follow her to the bedroom and grab up a handful of dirty clothes. One of my shirts is sopping wet and stinks like hops. I scowl at the damp spot staining the wood. "What the fuck happened here?"

"Sorry. I dropped the can," Luna says, and her cheeks flush.

"Don't worry about it. If you like beer, help yourself," I say, gathering up a few more dirty clothes from the floor. We've got to make this place look livable if we want her to stay. She's not the kind of woman who deserves to be fucked in the filth of our place.

Luna peels off my black sweatshirt and slides under the covers, and fucking hell, but I think I'm going to explode at the

146

sight of her pretty little body stretched out on my sheets, not a stitch of clothes on it. All that time, she didn't even have panties under the shirt. Her skin is milky white, her body emaciated but with just enough curves to say she's a woman, old enough to mate. Her mound is covered with a sleek pelt of hair, and her tight little tits are tipped with pink nipples just begging to be sucked. It's all I can do not to dive between her skinny thighs and suck that sweet pink pussy until she screams like a banshee.

"Warrick doesn't like me, does he?"

"Huh?" I yank my attention back to her mouth.

"Warrick. He doesn't like me." She tugs the covers over her luscious tits, hiding them from sight.

I blow out a lungful of air, trying to get the blood flowing from my little head back to the big one. "Don't worry about Warrick," I say. "He won't hurt you. His bark is worse than his bite."

She runs her hands over the bedspread, outlining her curves. "Why's he so mad?"

"What?" I say, wondering where that idea came from. "He's not mad. He looks scary because he *is* scary. He's a badass motherfucker. When he's on the back of his beast of a motorcycle, riding through town, people take one look at him and run for cover."

"But you said he wouldn't hurt me."

"He won't," I say. "He wouldn't hurt a defenseless pup like you."

"Oh," she says, settling back on the bed, seeming to relax at last.

"Do I scare you?" I ask, unable to help myself.

She pierces me with a beguiling gaze. "You did at first, but…" She shakes her head, and her long, silky hair musses against the pillowcase. "Not anymore. I like you."

Did she just say she liked me? Lucifer help me, I'm screwed. I can't recall a woman ever saying that to me. Women want to fuck me, and then they want to pretend they don't know me. They want to ride my dick until they've had three or four come-to-Jesus orgasms. They want to throw it in their exes face that they moved on with a bigger, meaner, tougher guy with a bigger dick. They don't *like* me.

Suddenly, it feels like I swallowed a fishhook and she's reeling me in. It fucks with my head, so after one final sweep of her blanketed body and her innocent face, I flick off the light and leave her to sleep. I've never wanted more from a woman than they want from me. I sure as fuck never wanted one to *like* me. That would just lead to even more trouble. But damn if Luna's words echoing in my head don't sound good.

Chapter Twelve

Luna

The days pass in a blur as I get to know the three men who took me in while trying not to be a burden, be polite, and not bring them down with my grief. Sometimes, the pain of losing Mama hits me fresh, and I have to go curl up in the bed and hope I won't wake up. I remember what she said about not trusting wolves, and also what they said about being outlaws, which is better than a pack and more trustworthy. Maybe they're right. These men don't seem so scary once I know them a little, though Warrick's always grumpy and watches me with as much suspicion as I have of him.

Over the next few days, Callan tends to me when I'm sad and makes sure I eat, Ethan teaches me how to wash the sheets so I can have a clean bed, and Warrick just watches when he's around. They all go off to "a job," which Ethan says is just another way of saying digging ditches, during most of daylight hours for a couple days. When they're gone, I clean up the messy house some and wash the clothes that are scattered everywhere.

A few mornings later, I'm dragged from sleep by the sound of the brothers' shouts. Sliding from the sheets, I stealth-walk across the bedroom and crack the door.

"We can't take care of another stray," Warrick roars. "She's a puppy in a wolf's body."

"But—" Callan starts.

Warrick cuts him off. "We have no idea why she was in that swamp. If she really lived there, she was probably on the run from something, which means that something is still out there, still after her. Which means she'll bring trouble straight here." A loud pounding rattles the air like Warrick is hammering the table with his fist. "Why should we put ourselves in danger for someone we don't even know?"

"We can protect her," Callan says. "If something's coming after her, she won't make it on her own. She can't defend herself. But we can."

"No, goddamn it," Warrick snarls. "She can't be trusted. She could be lying about everything. We have no proof that she even lost her mother. That could be just a story she told us to get sympathy."

The pain in my chest flares at the reminder of the constant ache of what I've lost. *Mama, gone. My home, abandoned.*

The scratch of the little stick Warrick uses to light the end of his roll of dried leaves crackles into the air. Then, the smell of the burning leaves tickles my nose.

"We can't keep her," Warrick says in a softer tone. "She's a liability to what we've made for ourselves here. For all we know, she's one of Axel's, come to catch us in the act."

I fling open the door and march out of the bedroom, my hands balled into fists by my side. They're in the kitchen sitting around the table. Three heads turn to stare at me as I march into the kitchen.

"Y'all think I'm lying about losing the only person in my life?" I demand.

With three sets of eyes glued to my body, I'm suddenly aware of how alone I am. They're each bigger than any one man ought to be, and they have the armor of ink on their skin and clothes on top of that. Most of all, they have each other, and being together makes them three times as strong as each man is alone.

I'm one little wolf, without even a set of clothes to call my own. I stand in the kitchen with all I have—my own body, which they're all three staring at like they'd like to gobble it down in one bite. I've never felt so small, so vulnerable, so much in need of someone on my side.

"You want me to go home, I'll go," I say. "I didn't ask you to bring me here. I never wanted to be a bother, but y'all told me to stay when I made to leave."

"You're not a bother," Callan says, standing and peeling off his t-shirt. His muscles ripple in waves under his skin as he hands me his shirt. I swallow, pulling my eyes away from the mesmerizing sight of all that strength and power in one body.

I pull on his shirt, grateful for the warmth and the comforting smell of my favorite brother surrounding me. I'm shaking, though I don't feel cold, and it helps soothe down my nerves.

"If you don't believe me, ask Healer Artuna," I say to Warrick. "Mama's dead body is still at her place if she hasn't fed it to the gators yet."

Ethan pushes back from the table and declares, "I think she's telling the truth."

Warrick sucks on the end of his rolled leaves and exhales a plume of smoke. "If you expect us to trust you, you'd better get to talking," he says. "You been a week, and we don't know the first thing about you. Who killed your mama? Why were you living in the swamp? What happened that left you lying in the swamp for dead? Who's after you?"

"You're upsetting her," Callan says, guiding me to a chair. "Let me get you some food, Luna, and we'll talk. We're happy to share what we got, but we'd like to get to know you better."

I nod, grateful for the moment to get my thoughts together. He delivers me a plate of meat and eggs, along with a cup of the bitter black water they drink. They call it coffee and drink it like it's water, though I can only drink half a cup of it before I start shaking and feeling like I might explode.

"Go on then," Ethan says, snagging the bag of leaves from Warrick. He starts making a little roll of them inside the paper they use while I talk.

"The only people I've ever met before you guys are the wolf pack," I say. "And that was just a few days ago, I think two days before you found me. Mama got attacked by a panther in the swamp, and then this awful wolf found me. She promised to help Mama if I came back to the pack with her. I knew not to trust her, but I didn't have a choice if I wanted to help Mama."

Callan scoots over and lays a hand on my leg. It's rough and hard on the palm, but his touch is gentle and sends warmth creeping up my thigh in a way that's too distracting.

"Go on," he says. "You're doing great, Luna."

I take a deep breath, gripping the fork to keep from shaking. "I went back with them, and this wolf named Axel said I'd be his True Mate. I sort of knew what it meant but not really, because it turns out it means he has to stab my heat with a meat stick called a cock, and then I got this mark."

I pull up the oversized sleeve of Callan's shirt and show them the mark, which glowed like a full moon the first night I got it. After it burst into flame, it was an angry blister, but after a quarter moon's worth of days have passed, it's only an angry red scar. The pain of the wound still hurts down deep in my soul when I look at it, though.

I drop the sleeve just in time to catch a look I don't understand passing between the men. Ethan's mouth is twitching. Callan is gazing at me with eyes that warm the cavity inside my chest but also make it ache. Warrick's brows are drawn together like he's even madder than usual. He sucks hard on his smoke stick, his eyes flashing with danger.

"And then what?" he asks, his voice a growl that makes me cringe instinctually.

"And then I didn't like that, so I ran away and met a vampire," I say. "But I guess that was the wrong thing to do because Axel was very mad when he found out I talked to him, and he said—" My voice catches, and my throat aches so bad I have to stop and hitch in a breath. "He said I was a traitor. That we couldn't be mates anymore."

A hot tear spills from my lashes and rolls down my cheek when I remember the shame and confusion of that moment. "And then," I choke out past the tears. "And then he brought a shaman to dissolve the bond, and her magic reached into my soul and ripped it out of my body, tearing me to shreds from the inside out."

I can't hold back the tears now, and they stream down my cheeks like angry brands, reminding me of the pain and shame of being rejected.

"Fucking hell," Ethan mutters, lighting the smoke stick he made. "This calls for more than breakfast. Get this chick a beer, and here, take my cigarette, Luna."

I shake my head, determined to get through this if only to walk away without letting Warrick think I'm a liar and a spy.

"The fates weren't done with me yet," I say, forcing back a sob. "I ran out of there and went to my mama, because even though I mostly take care of her, she still makes me feel cared for when I'm hurt, like she did when I was little. But when I got to the healer's, Mama died right there before my very eyes."

"Luna," Callan says, scooting closer. But I'm suddenly filled with anger at him, too. Not just Warrick, but Callan, who I know dragged me from the swamp.

I push away and jump to my feet, tearing off Callan's shirt and hurling it at his feet. "I just wanted to die," I say. "I didn't ask to be rescued. I don't *need* to be rescued. So you can go back to living your happy lives just like you were before, and you don't have to worry if you can trust me, because I won't be around to wonder about!"

By the time I finish, I'm sobbing and yelling at once. The pain of what happened crashes over me like ocean waves now that I had to say it out loud for all of them to hear, and shame fills me until I can't contain it anymore. So I turn and run out of the house, away from them, away from everything.

Chapter Thirteen

Luna

I race through the trees around the triplet's house, my head spinning with confusion. I don't remember coming here, and I haven't left since waking in their bed. I don't know where I am or how to get home. Nothing smells familiar. Nowhere feels safe. My shredded heart can't take the pain of life anymore.

I hear a snap of a twig and spin around. A huge, dark shape rockets across the carpet of pine needles, straight for me. I scream and start to shift into a wolf, but the shape blurs into a man and catches me before I can. He wraps his arms around me, the shock of his huge, hot body against mine knocking the breath from me and replacing it with pure panic. I writhe in his arms, screams tearing from me.

"Luna, stop," he commands fiercely. "It's just me."

I stop screaming when his words cut through my haze of panic, and I realize it's just Callan.

"Let me go!" I shove at his chest to no effect. He's as strong as he looks, like a tree has imprisoned me in its unbreakable limbs.

"Are you going to run?" His golden eyes captivate me.

"Of course I'm going to run!" I bite his shoulder, kicking my legs.

"Fucking stop, Luna," he snaps, his arms still wrapped tightly around me. "I'm not going to hurt you."

"You've already hurt me," I snap back.

His grip loosens instantly, but he doesn't release me. "We didn't know, pet," he says quietly. "I just need you to listen to me for a second. If you don't like what I have to say, you can run."

There's a warmth emanating from his eyes that does strange things to my insides, and being pressed up against him while neither of us are dressed makes a strange ache grow in my lower belly, like it did when Axel touched me in the shower.

I nod my head, and he releases his embrace and steps back, palms out, his feet making soft noises in the pine needles. He's huge like a giant, his thighs as powerful as top half of his body, and he has the same meat stick as Axel, but his hangs down instead of standing up. He's still close enough that his warmth touches me while the early morning sunlight filtering through the boughs softly lights his rugged features.

"Go on," I say, swallowing past a quivery feeling in my throat.

"We moved out here when the pack banished us, too," he says. "We got each other, and that's about it. Truth be told, we weren't looking to change that. But having you here for just a few days... Well, it shook us up, that's all."

I cross my arms across my chest, trying to hold back the tears that want to come again. "I don't want to cause problems. Not between the three of you. I know what it's like to have only one person you can count on. I wouldn't have liked anyone coming in and getting between me and Mama, either."

Callan shakes his head, his shaggy hair swaying in the breeze. "That won't happen," he says. "No one could ever come between us. Now Warrick, he don't trust easy, but I bet the two of you are more alike than either of you is willing to let on. He wasn't expecting you to turn our universe upside down, but that don't mean he doesn't need it the same as the rest of us."

"Need what?" I ask. "Shaking up?"

He gives me a crooked grin. "Yeah."

"What if I don't need it?" I ask.

"Well, pet, I think your world's already been shaken up," he says. "And we'd like to be the shelter from the storm for a while, if you'll have us. Thing is… We may not have realized it, but I think we needed someone like you to come along and remind us there's something in the world besides what we were used to getting."

"Like what?" I ask, utterly confused.

"Like you," he says softly, stepping closer.

My heart is suddenly doing its rabbit-run again. I swallow and lower my gaze to the bite mark I left on his shoulder, which seeps blood.

"But Warrick hates me," I whisper. "He doesn't want me here."

"He don't hate you," Callan says. "He needs you most."

I gulp, confused by all the funny sensations running through me, the thoughts and fears and hopes and desires in my head banging up against the way my body feels warm and languid when he's near, like I need to lie down and sun myself and have a dream I can't remember afterwards.

"You can't blame us for going a little nuts when you showed up," Callan says. "I mean…you're a fucking gorgeous woman. Of course it takes some adjusting to having you living under our roof, walking around like that…" His eyes roam over my body, and my nipples stiffen like they want some attention.

"What does that matter?" I say, inching toward him.

He places his palms on my shoulders and rubs them up and down. I want to lean into him, to have his strong arms around me again, holding me like he did before. This time, I wouldn't fight. I'd pay attention and really feel his huge body wrapped around my small one, all our skin pressed together.

"It doesn't matter what you look like," Callan says, and I see that funny lump on his neck bob up and down, like he's trying to swallow something that's stuck there. "Listen, Luna… We've had our share of hardships, but none of us can imagine what it's like to be severed from a True Mate. Most wolves don't have one, so we can't know. It's a rare and precious thing, and usually the only separation is if one of the pair dies. No one in his right mind would sever the bond intentionally."

My voice cracks when I speak. "Then why did Axel?"

Callan's hands curl into fists. "Because he's a fucking bastard, that's why."

No one has ever defended me before. Mama would've if she'd had the wits about her to do it, but she just didn't understand things the same way I did. If there was a storm coming or a gator on our hillock, I was the one who prepared our home or chased off the predators. I protected us and fought for survival for the both of us.

But this man standing in front of me seems to want to protect me, even though I don't understand why. Something flutters down in my belly like the wings of a swarm of bats catching skeeters over the swamp. I don't understand that, either.

"So, what do you say, pet?" Callan asks. "Let us take care of you for a while, at least? I already admitted we need it, and I think you need us, too."

I feel a smile tugging at my mouth, and I can't get it to go away even when I bite on the corner of my lip. "Okay," I say at last, nodding my head.

Callan lets out a whoop and dives at me, scooping me up over his shoulder and pumping a fist in the air. A giggle bursts from me, and I clap my hand over my mouth, feeling like I shouldn't laugh so soon after Mama died. But he took me by surprise, and he's laughing, too. He turns and runs back toward their house, carrying me over his shoulder. I must have made a good choice, because I feel just about as happy as he is about it.

Maybe there's hope after all. Maybe there can be life after Mama. When Axel banished me, I felt like I wasn't worth being his mate, but now I know I was wrong. And he was wrong. There are other people in the world who want me even if he doesn't.

Chapter Fourteen

Luna

The moon goes from full to new by the time I'm properly settled into the triplets' house. About half the days, they all go off to what they call a job, which Ethan explains is really just a way to make money, which is something everyone apparently needs, though I don't really understand why. I understand trading, but I can't quite grasp why everyone agrees that green paper is important and that everything else can be traded for it.

Nonetheless, I'm able to learn so much that every night, my brain feels like it will burst with all the new information and knowledge. I try to hold it all in, scared some of it will slip away and I'll make a mistake like I did with the vampire, and that the triplets will reject me, too.

One evening when Callan is in the middle of cooking, blasting the radio in the kitchen, and Warrick is hiding away in his room, I hear yelling outside. I jump up from the couch and run outside into the sultry evening air.

Ethan's on the ground on top of a guy, pummeling him with his fists.

My heart jumps. Is it Axel, my True Mate, coming back for me? Does the inside of his ribs still ache when he thinks about me, like mine do when I think of him?

Then, my belly tightens into knots. Of course it's not Axel. He didn't want me. He wouldn't come back for me.

I raise my head and sniff the air, but the only smells I catch are Ethan's potent, musky fragrance and a hint of ash that reminds me of the man in the woods with the very clean house, who gave me tainted water. *Evan.*

"Whatever you think I did, I didn't fuck your woman," Ethan hollers between blows. "I don't fuck dead things."

So, he is a vampire.

"Liar," the other man screeches, his fists moving in a blur as he rains blows on my huge wolf friend. I can see it's not Evan, though. His hair and skin are pale.

"Who you calling a liar, you slimy leech?" Ethan roars, hauling back and letting loose with another bone-cracking assault.

Blood spurts from the guy's mouth, and he clocks Ethan in the forehead with his skull. Ethan's hands fly to his head, which gives the vampire enough purchase to wrench his body out from underneath Ethan.

"Ethan!" I cry, sprinting toward him. I throw myself in front of him and throw out my arms, like I can block Ethan's hulking form from attack.

Ethan stumbles to his feet, puts his arm around me, and grins. "See, you got the wrong guy," he tells the vampire. "This here's my lady. I was with her that night. Isn't that right, darlin'?" He leans down and kisses the top of my head.

I know I should agree, so I nod. After all, Ethan's been home every night I've lived here... Though sometimes not until I'm asleep. I know he's home part of the night, though, because he's at breakfast every morning. "That's right," I say to the vampire. "He was with me all day and all night."

Ethan makes an odd purring rumble and pulls me closer. "Yep, we were together *all* night."

The vampire, a tall man with no muscles and too-pale hair, lurches to his feet and studies us for a few seconds—first me, and then Ethan, and then back to me.

"You're lying," he snarls. He lunges for Ethan, who whisks me out of the way. But that only gives the vampire a direct shot, and the man leaps onto Ethan's back and sinks long canines into the side of his neck. I want to jump in, but I don't want to distract Ethan again and give the vampire more chances to hurt him.

I bolt into the house, screaming for his brothers.

Warrick emerges from his bedroom, a thunderous frown on his face. "What's with all the caterwauling?" he demands. "Are Callan and Ethan squabbling like usual?"

"Come quick," I cry. "A vampire's biting Ethan!"

"What?" Warrick starts for the front door, bellowing as he goes. "Callan! Where the fuck are you?"

A second later, Callan rushes from the kitchen. "What is it?"

"Stay with Luna," Warrick orders. "I gotta beat some skulls in."

He charges out the door on his bare feet.

I rush toward the window, my heart flipping in my chest. All the loss and fear I've experienced floods through my bloodstream. My fingers curl around the windowsill, gaining a few splinters.

In the yard outside, grunts and groans erupt from the men as they assault one another with fists and feet.

"Is Ethan going to be okay?" I ask, not tearing my eyes from the three men outside.

Callan's warm palms land on my shoulders, and he pivots me toward him. "You don't need to worry about my big, bad brothers."

"What if they get hurt?" I demand, straining my neck to witness the violence happening outside.

"They won't." Callan forcefully guides me across the room, heading toward the sofa. He plunks me down and crouches before me, resting his hands on my knees. We've all chipped in and cleaned up around the house, and there are no longer clothes and beer bottles everywhere. Now, there's just a mattress on the floor where Ethan sleeps.

I start to get up, but Callan gently presses me back.

"We can take care of ourselves, pet," he assures me.

"He bit Ethan's neck," I say, the shock still sitting heavy in my belly.

Callan places a fingertip to my lips. "Shhh. Everything's going to be okay, pet. I promise."

"I just can't lose someone else," I say, trying to sound determined. The quaver in my voice gives away my fear, though.

Callan slides up onto the sofa beside me and slides a protective arm around me. "Tell me a story," he says, smiling down at me.

"What?" I look up at him, blinking.

"Tell me what you liked most about living in Bogbeast Waters."

"Oh…" My stupid eyes almost fill with tears as I recall what it was like living there with my Mama, but I hold them back and think of the good times. "I loved the moon shining over the honey locusts and tupelo trees," I start. Callan smiles and nods encouragingly, so I go on. "I loved chasing the swamp rabbits and catching them for supper. The sand cranes were kind of fun. I'd chase them in my wolf form, though I never caught them. Just watching them take to the sky was worth it, though."

The sounds of the struggle float through the window—there's a whack and a clang, followed by a soft thud. Then, swishing noises and grunts.

Callan squeezes my shoulder, pulling me closer. "What else?"

Wistful feelings swirl through my heart as I go back there in my mind. "There was a spring near our place. We'd head out there in the evening and soak a while. Sometimes when Mama's mind wandered off, I'd bring her out there to keep an eye on her, just letting her soak while I'd wash the clothes."

"Your mama wasn't right in the head?"

"I don't know," I say honestly. "I never knew different, just that we didn't think the same. I know her True Mate was murdered, and her soul snapped. Then she took me out there to protect me. I've been taking care of her ever since I was little, though. Protecting us both." Sniffling, I wipe my eyes with the back of my hand.

Callan stares at me, his eyes wide. Then he clears his throat and says, "That's real sad, Luna. I'm sorry you had to do that."

I shrug. "It was hard, but we all got hard times, right? That's what Mama always said if I complained."

"I guess so," Callan says. "Can't say we haven't run into our share, too."

"What were your hard times?" I ask, snuggling even closer, wanting to share his stories, too. His face hardens into lines and shadows, and I think I did something wrong. When I stiffen, ready to be scolded, though, he pulls me closer, setting me on his knee.

"The kind where your old man lives in a vial of goblin blood, and he beats the shit out of you just because you're still breathing," he says.

"Oh, no," I say, laying my fingers against his rugged cheek with the bristling of short, black fur. "Why would he do that?"

"Goblin blood is real addictive and makes a man real mean," he says. "He took out his rage on us and our poor Ma, too. We left as soon as we turned sixteen. Been on our own almost ever since."

"That makes us kindred spirits," I say, placing a hand on his shoulder and gazing into his green-flecked eyes.

Callan's throat-lump bobs up and down, and he looks like he might bolt if I wasn't on his lap. His gaze drops to my lips, and a little bat-wing thumps against my heart.

At the sound of pounding footsteps, Callan quickly pushes me off his knee and back onto the couch cushion.

"Told you it would all work out," he says with a grin.

Warrick and Ethan stroll through the front door, arms around one another's shoulders, laughing. I can feel the dominating maleness of their energy, some rawness in their scent ramped up by the fight. I sniff the air, and Ethan grins.

"You like the smell of that testosterone, huh?" he asks with a wink. "I know a way we can make more of that."

His face is bloody and bruised, and crimson drips down his neck from where the vampire bit him.

"How?" I ask.

Warrick throws a sharp jab into Ethan's ribs, and the long-haired wolf groans. I know by now that they hit each other a lot, and that it doesn't mean they're mad or fighting. Callan says that's how they play.

"Is the vampire gone?" I ask.

The two men side-eye each other and grin.

"Yeah. Sure. He's gone," Warrick says, followed by more chuckles. He's got a swelling on his lip that's leaking blood, along with scrapes and bruises on both cheeks.

My forehead furrows in a crease. "Why are you laughing?"

"You know what?" Callan says, pushing to stand. "I should help Ethan get cleaned up, make sure that vampire bite is clean. It may take a while."

"There's some yard work yet to do," Warrick says, even though it's almost dark out, and they usually come in from working by now.

I narrow my eyes when they all glance at one another, sharing some secret that I'm not a part of. They do this a lot— casting glances at one another, laughing at things I don't understand, disappearing outside or suddenly leaving to take a shower. If anyone's not to be trusted, it's them.

"Do you want me to leave?" I ask, standing on stiff legs.

Ethan cups his hand around my jaw and tips my face up. "That's the last thing we want, pup."

His face looks awful. I reach out and gently stroke one of the bruises beneath his stubble. He rubs his face into my touch and closes his eyes, inhaling so deep his nostrils flare.

"I just got to get cleaned up," he says, his voice gruff but gentle. "And then we got a few things to take care of."

Staring into his golden-green gaze is like peering through the morning mist over the swamp when the sun hit it just right. My tension dissolves, and I nod my head.

"Tell you what," Warrick says. "I've got to run into town and grab a few things. Luna, you'll come with me. Might be good for you to get out of the house and do something. If you're gonna stay on a while, you need your own things, anyway. Clothes and the like. Lady stuff." He looks away, rubbing his jaw, and the other two chuckle.

"You want to take me into town?" I ask, my heartbeat picking up speed. "Just us?"

Warrick barely talks to me, and we're never alone together. If the other two are out, he goes to his room and closes the door. The others teach me things, let me help them cook or clean up, and talk to me like I'm one of them when we all go out on the porch after supper and have a beer together. Warrick only watches. Though he never speaks directly to me unless he has to, sometimes I feel his gaze and turn to see him silently watching me with an unreadable expression. Despite Callan saying otherwise, I know Warrick doesn't like me or want me here.

But he hasn't hurt me when we were alone, and he hasn't told me to leave. If he meant to hurt me, he could have. And now he's inviting me to go to town with him, something Mama never let me do. Maybe this will be my chance to change his mind about me.

"Aww, the pup's scared of you," Ethan says, slugging Warrick's arm. "I told you to be nicer to her."

Warrick only grunts and turns to me, jerking his thumb toward the door. "Let's go."

Chapter Fifteen

Warrick

Luna trails behind me as I stride from the house, heading for my custom-designed motorcycle. The salt air is kissing it into a bucket of rust, but nothing to do about that in these parts. My brothers and I worked on my baby for a solid year, testing and perfecting each change until we hit the sweet spot. She's a vintage Harley, chopped low and mean like me. A chrome skull and crossbones leer from the handlebars, and the engine's a loud growl, warning shifters and humans alike to get the fuck out of the way, 'cause I'm going to blow through them, past them or over them. The frame's been converted to a rigid hardtail, we added eight inches to the frame tube, and the steering neck rake is set at an angle of forty-five degrees.

When I pull the motorcycle out of the garage and lean it on the kickstand, Luna climbs on the front. I bark out a laugh. Does she think I'm going to sit on the Queen seat?

"You driving, sweetheart?" I say, towering over her. "You're in the King's seat."

She gazes up at me with the eyes of a deer in a hunter's sight. "I thought this was the seat."

She chews on her lower lip, a picture of nervous innocence. I stare at her mouth, and a temporary insanity takes over because the next second I'm wondering what it would be like if *I* were to nibble on her lower lip... And work my way down to other places on her tight little body.

What the fuck is wrong with me?

I'll take a bang piece now and then, but it's a "needs met and see ya later" kind of arrangement, not a tasting party. When I think about it, it's been a while since I screwed a chick. Probably why my cock is twitching in my jeans even though Luna's nothing like my regular rough-around-the-edges shifter-groupie type. I need a woman who knows what she's doing—and what she's getting. There are always human women lining up for a chance to ride a wolf cock, but they know they won't get more than that and they aren't looking for it. It's a certain type of woman who gets wet for men like us, and that type is the exact opposite of the little wolf pup straddling my bike.

Cleaning up Ethan's messes when his cock socks get clingy, or their men start fights with him for sleeping with their women, has taught me that pussy's usually more trouble than it's worth. Not even going to look at the one living under my roof. Luna's nothing but a PYT—way too young and inexperienced for the likes of me. I'd destroy her. I'm probably twice her age, not to mention that though her body might be prime and ready for fucking, her mental age leaves a few years to be desired.

With a grunt, I say, "Get off."

She obediently climbs from the black leather seat. I swing my leg over, place my boots on the ground and my hands on the handlebars. "Get behind me," I say, jerking my head backward to indicate her place. "That's the Queen's seat."

She climbs on. "Am I the Queen?"

"Hang on," I say, powering on the bike and revving the engine. "And put your feet there." I indicate the chrome footrests on either side.

She carefully positions each foot in the right place. "What do I hold onto?" she shouts over the roar.

"Whatever you can get your hands around," I say with a chuckle. Damn, she's going to freak the fuck out when I take off. Bastard that I am, I can't wait. I crank up the engine and release the brake. We rocket along the dirt road, fishtailing as I let the bike find its rhythm.

Luna screams and clutches my leather vest.

I laugh at her fear because I'm a dick like that, and then I increase the speed just to hear her shriek again. Instead, her screams turn into whoops and laughter that joins mine, and her arms slide around me, tightening their hold. The chick has some *cojones.*

We power through the trees, sending a gator waddling for the water to avoid getting beheaded by my front tire. I'm digging Luna's exuberance until she pushes her pussy into my lower back from her slightly raised position. And then she slides her hands between my legs, right next to my cock. She's impressed me that she's having fun instead of being scared, as I expected, but I guarantee fun time is over if Daddy comes out to play.

I scoot her hands onto my thighs one at a time with my gloved hand and give each one a solid pat, indicating they stay put right where they are. But my cock has taken notice of the attention and starts stirring in my jeans again. I can feel her warm little paws on my thighs, so close to wrapping around my shaft and...

I shut down that line of thinking real quick, but I've got a massive hard-on until we reach the edge of town. Then I focus on what I'm doing instead of the skinny little body wrapped around mine. I slow things down and set the bike to cruise. I like to take it nice and slow when I hit Jacksonville and watch people scurry to get out of my way.

Some of the local shifters glare at me. One asshole even flips me off, which makes me chuckle. There's not a damn shifter or human in these parts who could get me to piss my pants in fear—they're the ones who would wet themselves if I even glance in their direction.

We pull up to Paradise Acres, and I park the bike on the cracked pavement. There are raised lines of paint where the parking spots used to be marked, but they're faded the same color as the rest of the lot, and no one uses them. We just park wherever the fuck we see space between sinkholes and potholes for whatever we're driving.

Luna simply sits there with her damn pussy pressed into my sweat-soaked back.

I exhale a sigh. "This is the part where you get off the bike."

"Oh," she says and withdraws her hands and pussy, scrambling off the motorcycle.

I climb off, remove the key and shove it in my pocket. I know my bike will be safely parked—no one dares to lay a fucking finger on my ride unless they have an upcoming funeral planned.

"I've been there," Luna says brightly, pointing to a weirdo shop for supernatural potions and beauty bullshit.

"I thought you lived in the woods and had never met a human before." I slow my gait so she can keep up with my long-legged stride. The sidewalk's radiating heat from the intense sun, and I'm ready to get inside the artificial cool of a store for a few minutes.

"It was only a few days ago," Luna mumbles. "When I was being prepped for Axel."

"Don't you worry about Axel, sweetheart," I say, ruffling the top of her head. "His expiration date will come soon enough."

Her hair's a tangled mess from the wind, and a scowl bruises her pretty face.

I don't have a clue what the frown's about, but I shrug it off and steer her away from Lewis's shop and toward *Better Buy Big Box* store. "That's the store we want."

When we get to the front door, it glides open, and we're met with a blast of cool air. We trek inside with Luna looking this way and that like a pie-eyed child.

"Just get whatever you think you'll need," I say, sweeping my hand around the super-sized store. "And meet me at the register in fifteen."

She shakes her head and wraps her arms around herself like the AC makes her cold instead of being a fucking blessing. "I don't need anything."

"Yes, you do," I say, grabbing her wrist. I seize a metal cart and shove it at her. "If you can't get your shit yourself, we'll stick together. You push."

Her brow furrows, and she examines the cart, the wheels, everything. "Well, ain't this something?" she asks at last. "I wish I'd had one of these when I killed a gator. I could have pushed it home instead of dragging it by the tail."

The thought of her dragging a five-hundred-pound alligator through the bog tickles my funny bone, and I can't help but laugh. "Yeah, babe, you could have pushed him home through the swamp."

Resting a hand on her shoulder, I turn her toward the women's clothes. I have no idea what size she wears, but her shoulder feels delicate under my calloused paw. In the clothes section, I hold up a few things that look practical and the right size, letting her approve the ones she likes before I toss them in the cart.

When we're done, I gesture to the personal care section. "Do you need your own shampoo and shit?"

"No," she says. "I like yours. It makes me smell like you."

Not going to touch that jerk-off grenade.

The next aisle is the toiletries aisle. A woman in that section takes one look at me, drops the basket she's carrying, and scurries away.

Good. We can use the privacy. I scan the woman's abandoned basket and note several items that Luna will need— a toothbrush, deodorant, razors and shaving cream, and tampons. I dump the contents of her abandoned basket into our cart and decide we're done.

"What is all this stuff?" Luna asks, picking up the deodorant.

Christ. I forget she's lived like a savage her whole life.

"That's so you don't stink."

"I stink?" she asks, her eyes widening.

"You smell fine," I grit out, resisting the urge to take in a lungful of her scent. It's bad enough to have her always padding around the house on her cute little bare feet, leaving her womanly scent everywhere she curls up. I won't let my brain follow that train of thought to the logical next station—what she might taste like.

She picks up the package of razors. "And this?"

"Some men like it when you shave the hair off your legs." The devil whispers in my ear, so I add, "And when you shave the hair between them."

Luna's face twists into a frown. "You don't like my hair?"

"Real men don't mind real women," I say. "Hair and all. But sometimes you might want to be smooth and soft for him. Just to change it up."

She nods and reaches into the cart for the toothbrush. "I don't need this. I share Ethan's toothbrush."

"You can have your own damn toothbrush," I grit out, an irrational annoyance with my brother grinding into me. It's not like he was sharing a dildo. And now I'm fucking thinking about whether Luna masturbates, and whether she needs a sex toy to keep her satisfied. The rest of us have been jerking off like teenagers since she moved in.

"Go," I snap, and she obediently resumes pushing the cart. We wander up the aisle, heading for the checkout stand, and I spy some hairbrushes. I toss one at her, and she deftly catches it.

"I've used one of these," she says. "You could use one, too. All of you. Can we share this kind of brush?"

"We don't need a goddamn girl's hairbrush," I snap. I'm starting to not like this experience. I'm not afraid of anything or anyone, but this sweet little barely legal scrap of ass is getting me flustered.

"Oh, look!" She grabs a box of purple hair dye and holds it up so I can see the smiling woman pictured. "Ama said I can't put color in my hair, but look how pretty this is."

"Ama's a bitch," I say, pitching the box of dye into the cart. "You should do what you want and have some fun—if you even know what that is."

"Thanks!" she says, and she flashes me a smile that threatens to make me hard all over again. The day when a smile can make my dick hard is the day I really need to pound some pussy before I do something stupid.

I increase my pace.

She scampers after me, only to get in line behind the same woman who ran when she saw us coming. She glances nervously between me and Luna, a fretful stitch in her brow and her foot tapping nervously as the cashier scans her items. She probably thinks I've kidnapped Luna to turn her into a club whore.

"What about these?" Luna asks, reaching into the cart and fishing out the box of tampons.

"Not my place to tell you," I say. "You'll figure it out."

"How can I figure it out if you won't tell me?"

"Ask Callan," I say, flashing her an evil smile. Let him deal with her feminine problems. He's the one who dragged her home.

"Why does Callan know if you don't? Does he use these and not you?"

The woman in front of us yanks her bags from the cashier, shooting us looks of disgust and abject pity before stomping off.

"No, he doesn't use those," I say to Luna. "He's a *man*. You use tampons when it's your... Moon cycle." I'm starting to sweat in this frigid, ice-chilled store. I shoot her a meaningful look, trying to shut her up, and shove a handful of clothes onto the counter.

"My moon cycle?" Her brow stitches together. "Ohhh. You mean when I'm bleeding."

"Right. That."

The cashier is a young, pimply-faced kid, barely out of diapers if his whisker-free chin is any indication.

Luna's still clutching the damn box of tampons. "What do I do with them?"

"We pay for all this shit and leave," I say, batting the box onto the counter.

It's official. I've been unmanned by this pipsqueak of a girl, and I don't like it—not one bit. I don't know what I can do about it except to climb back on my motorcycle and resist the sensation of her hot pussy pressed against my lower back as I take our stray back home where I'll blow my load in the shower, picturing her skinny legs spread wide and my thick cock wrecking her tight little cunt.

Chapter Sixteen

Callan

It takes the better part of an hour to cleanse and tend Ethan's wounds. That vampire did a number on him, barely missing his carotid artery, or I'd be a twin now, instead of a triplet.

Bloody towels fill the kitchen sink, and crimson spatters cover the floor, but at least my brother is alive.

I had to break out our best liquor to stitch Ethan up good and proper. Now that he's shit-faced, I tie off the last thread on his neck and pat his shoulder. "Good as new."

Ethan opens his eyes—he's kept them squeezed shut with a grimace on his face while I've stitched his neck. "You fucking done?"

"Just about." I grab the can of spray antiseptic we keep for moments like this and spritz some onto his wound. "The scar'll leave you uglier than you already are. Want to see?"

Ethan takes another swig of whiskey and shakes his head. "Nah. I trust you."

"Then let's go deal with the body."

Pushing to his feet, he winces. "Damn. That fucking hurts." He lifts his hand and touches my artistry sewn into his flesh. A whistle leaves his lips. "Hoo, baby, I thought I was a goner there for a minute. But, damn, that was fun."

I place the medical supplies back in the canvas kit and shove it back in the cupboard where we keep it.

"We're going to have to wash all this shit," Ethan says, moving right past the mess. "After we deal with the dead guy."

"By 'we,' you mean 'me,' right?" I kick a red-streaked towel out of my path as we head toward the back door.

Ethan grunts. "Someone's gotta do it."

"It's your blood," I remind him.

"You're better at it than me," he says, nudging the screen door with the toe of his shit-kickers. The door flies open and whacks against the wall. Ethan exits, and I catch the door before it pops me in the face.

"You know how to do your own fucking laundry."

Ethan turns to grin over his shoulder at me. "We could teach Luna to do it."

"Fuck you. She's not our maid," I say, following him toward the trees lining our property.

"She could be," he counters. "I wouldn't mind seeing her on her hands and knees."

"Your dick's going to get you killed one of these days."

"Hey, we all have jobs. Why not give her one? I mean, if you don't want her cleaning up after us, I can think of another job she could do on her hands and knees."

I ignore him and storm ahead, trying to erase the image he put in my brain. Being outside always calms me. I love where we live, though maybe not the mosquitoes and chiggers that bite the shit out of us. The land on the edge of the swamp is a magical place. I love the smell of the cypress trees, the wildflowers and herbs that grow around here, even the smell of the swamp itself. Humans think the swamp stinks, but unless you're mucking around in it, stirring up the gasses and decaying matter, it's got a scent all its own, like wild things live here. And they're right.

Wild things is exactly what we are.

"Where the fuck did you stash the body?" I ask as we tromp deeper into the brush. The sun has sunk below the trees, but it's still light enough to see. Just the time of night the mosquitos come swarming.

"Oh, we dragged him some way out. Didn't want Miss Luna to see the carnage."

"What did you do to the guy?" I ask, stepping over a fallen log.

"I didn't do shit to *him*." He side-eyes me and waggles his eyebrows. "But I did leave his woman in a satisfied state of mind."

I shake my head and pick my way through some muddy terrain. "When will you learn that sometimes it's better to keep it in your pants?"

"This cock is meant for pleasure. Why waste a good thing?" He grabs his dick through his jeans and then pauses, pointing to a cluster of flies swirling around some bushes. "There he is."

I wave the flies away before lifting the Fetterbush branches before us. The corpse lays in a mangled heap, barely recognizable.

"Fuck, he stinks."

"Right?" Ethan says. "It's a wonder Frank hasn't found him. I thought we'd feed him to that old son of a bitch."

"Good idea," I say, grabbing the ankles of the body and hauling him out to where I can look at him. The dude's chest is torn apart like a wolverine got to him. "Shit."

Ethan chuckles. "You have to kill these motherfuckers with wood, so we used an old wooden spoon."

"You know you don't have to use wood if you just tear his head off, right?"

His chuckles turn into a raucous laugh. "Where's the fun in that?"

I stare at the dude's bashed-in skull. "You used a wooden spoon to bash in his head?"

"We used the shovel to bash in his head," Ethan corrects me. "Once he was down, I grabbed the old spoon I saw in the shed the other day and carved open his chest cavity."

"Where's the heart?"

"Warrick ate it," Ethan says, watching me heft the vampire's remains over my shoulder.

"He gagged down the whole heart?" I ask as we trudge toward the water. The stench of dead vamp fills my nostrils, and I'm more than ready to dump the body and be done with it.

"You know vamp blood only makes us stronger," Ethan says. When we get close to the swamp, he whistles. "Here, Frank, come get supper."

A set of eyes sinks into the reddish water, and ripples stream in our direction. A few seconds later, the oldest, meanest alligator in these parts waddles onto the shore, looking at us speculatively.

"Here, boy…catch," Ethan says.

I hurl the dead vamp, and it soars through the air and lands in a heap near Frank's seventy or so sharp teeth. I blow out a lungful of air and wipe the sweat from my neck and face.

My brother and his goddamned conquests…

As Frank goes to town on the body, dragging it to wherever he's going to consume it, Ethan and I head back toward the house.

"You been keeping your mitts to yourself with Luna, right?" I ask, sporting for a fight after hauling another one of Ethan's sexual messes through the woods.

"I can neither confirm nor deny," Ethan says with a smirk. He lifts a branch and holds it for me to trek past.

I swat his hand aside. "She's too young for you," I snap. "And too sweet to deserve your twisted ass fucking her up."

"Says who?" He gives me a shove.

"You do recall what we just did, right?" I shove him back, and he stumbles, nearly tripping over a branch in his drunken state.

"So?" he says hotly.

"So? That's the best you can come up with?" I throw my hands up and stomp back toward the cabin.

He charges after me and grabs my arm. "You're just pissed because *you* want her."

I yank my arm from his grip. "What I want is not to have to dispose of any dead bodies after you've fucked her and fucked her up."

"She doesn't have a boyfriend. She's fair game." Ethan's eyes are intense and heated, like he's been struggling to stay away from her, same as me.

"If anyone gets her, it's Warrick. He's our Alpha."

Ethan thunders after me again, but he doesn't argue. We storm toward the house like a couple dickheads about to get into a brawl over a piece of ass, which is exactly what we are.

To my surprise, he pulls up short at the house. "You're right," he says. "She deserves better than what any of us have to offer. She's way too young and innocent for the likes of us. We'd ruin her."

"And after what she's already been through with Axel," I remind him. "She needs someone to look after her, not sniff around seeing what he can get out of her."

He sighs, looking downright dejected. "Yeah, okay. I'll try to think of her instead of my dick when she's around."

"There's still a whole city full of women you can fuck," I say, gesturing vaguely toward Jacksonville.

He sighs again. "Yeah, I reckon."

"Then it's settled," I say, holding out a hand in a peace offering. "Neither of us stick our dicks in our houseguest. She's too naïve to know what's what. She needs our protection. We can't take advantage of her like that."

I don't know what it is about her, but she brings out some primal instinct in me. Yeah, that one, too. Of course I want to fuck her. I'm not blind. But more than that, I want to protect her, to erase what that asshole Axel did to her. And if I can't do that, then at least I can work to make her see that not all wolves are the traitorous sort she believes us to be. I want to work to get the wariness out of her eyes and put happiness there instead. After the life she's led, she deserves it.

Ethan grumbles, but he shakes on it. We may not be upstanding citizens, but our word is good—at least to each other.

Luna is officially off-limits.

Chapter Seventeen

Luna

Warrick barely says a word to me after we leave Paradise Acres. He drives me to something called a drive-through and buys me food he says is fast. The burger tastes okay, but the meat would be better if it wasn't cooked. The best part is a chocolate milkshake, which is unlike anything I've ever had in the swamp, that's for sure.

After we eat, Warrick tosses all the paper wrappers and the waxy cups in a bin and heads for his motorcycle. I follow obediently and climb on behind him, careful to keep my hands to myself, unless he careens around a turn, laying the bike on edge. Then, I grab on.

When he first started driving, it scared me, but once I realized it was just like running as a wolf but faster and louder, exhilaration poured through me. On the way home, I keep my exuberance to myself, though, since Warrick seems to be in one of his grumpy moods. When Mama got like that, it was best to shut my trap and let her come out of it herself.

When we get back to their house, he jerks his head and says, "Get your shit out of my saddlebags."

I climb down and unbuckle the shiny clasps on the black leather bag. After pulling the bags from the store free, I give him a big smile, hoping to cheer him up. I want him to feel as happy as I do right now.

"Thank you," I say. "I had a great time."

"Welcome," he grumbles. "Tell the boys I'm off to hunt."

I perk up at that. I haven't hunted since I left the swamp.

"Want company?" I ask, but the question is drowned by the roar of his bike, and then he's gone in a cloud of dust.

Whatever Callan was cooking, I'm glad I wasn't around for it, because it doesn't smell too good in the house. I can barely breathe over the chemical scent. The noise of the washing machine running echoes from the back room. Callan is on his knees, scrubbing the floor, which consists of big squares in black and white. A blue bucket full of water sits by his side, green plastic hand-shaped things cover his hands, and pinkish water pools around his knees.

He pauses when I enter, sitting up and dipping his scrubbing brush into the water. "Like my gloves?" he says, lifting the brush and wiggling the fingers of his free hand at me.

"Is that what those are?"

"Don't want to get dishpan hands," he says with a smile.

My brow furrows, and I ask the question I've said a hundred times a day since I arrived. "What is that?"

"When your skin gets all wrinkly from being in the water too long," he says. "How was your outing?"

I heft the bags in each hand. "We got a lot of stuff. What should I do with it?"

"Set it on the table. We'll figure out where to put it a soon as I'm done here." He gets back to cleaning, and I saunter over to the wooden table and drop the sacks on top. We've all been keeping the house a lot tidier than it was when I moved in, so there's room on the table now. The wood is shiny and smells like lemons after Callan showed me how to polish it the other day. But the lemon smell is overpowered by the horrible scent permeating the room.

"What's that awful smell?" I say, waving my hand in front of my nose.

"It sucks to have a sensitive wolf nose right about now," Callan says. "This is bleach. It's the only thing I could think of to get the bloodstains off the floor."

"Is Ethan okay?" I ask, sitting my backside on one of the chairs.

"Other than a bad hangover, he'll be fine by tomorrow." Callan grabs a pink-stained towel and wipes the water and bleach from the floor. Then, he hucks everything into the bucket and stands.

"What's a bad hangover?"

"That's what happens when you drink too much booze."

"Beer is booze," I say. "Ethan said it makes you happy."

"Right," Callan says. "But too much happiness from liquor can make you sick."

A thumping noise comes from the back of the house, the one that Callan says happens when you put too many clothes in the washing machine at once. I made the mistake a few times in my first few days, when we were trying to get the house in order.

"Shit," Callan says. "I've got to adjust the towels in the washer. I'll go empty this bucket, fix the towels, and be right back, okay?"

When he's gone, I fish out the purple hair color. I can't wait to try it out.

Callan strides back into the kitchen and grins at me. "What do you think?" he says, sweeping his arm in front of him. "Good as new?"

"Looks great," I say, returning the grin. I like being around someone who isn't always an explosion in the making. "Even cleaner than before we left. But I'd rather smell blood than that bleach."

"It's pretty bad," Callan says. "Want to go out on the porch while we look at your haul?"

He must see my blank expression because he gestures to the bags to let me know what he means. He grabs them off the table, and I follow him onto the porch, where we sit down on the wooden swing. Callan ducks inside and emerges with two beers, which he pops open with his lighter before handing me one and settling beside me.

"What'd you get?" he asks, crossing his ankle over his knee and sitting back with his beer. My eyes move over his relaxed posture, his muddy boots and dirty jeans, the sleeveless shirt that shows the bulging muscles of his arms, his skin wrapped with tattoos. A funny flutter presses down low in my belly, the way it did when I was on Warrick's bike. I wish I could press the feel-good place between my legs against him, like I did against Warrick's back.

"Well?" Callan says. "You going to show me or just stare at me all night?"

I tap my ragged nails on the arm of the swing and look away. "Warrick's pissed at me again."

"Oh, pet, don't take it personal," he says. "He acts like a prick around most people. It's just who he is."

I nod, though it seems like that's not a very happy way to live. I'll have to think of something I can do to make him happier, especially after all they've done for me. I've already helped clean the house, but that's only the start. If they're going to take such good care of me, I should take care of them, too.

Callan takes a swig of his beer, and his gaze lands on the hair color in my hands. "What's that you got there?"

I let him take the box of hair color while I take a drink of the cold, bitter beer. At first, I didn't like it much, but I'm starting to change my mind. It's cool on the hot evenings, and it makes me feel like I belong when we all sit out here together with a bottle, even though I usually only have one while they each have four or five.

"That will make me look like her," I say, leaning over Callan's arm and pointing to the girl on the box. "Isn't she pretty?"

"You want purple hair?" he asks, leaning back to peer down at my face.

"I've only ever had this color," I say, picking up a lock of hair. "I didn't know you could choose different colors. I guess Mama chose this one for me and forgot to tell me I could change it. But I think I might like to try every color before I pick one."

"Every color, huh," Callan says, taking another swig of beer and handing back the box. He has that shine in his eyes like he might laugh soon.

My neck and cheeks heat up. "I told Warrick that Ama said it was stupid, and he said, 'Ama's a bitch,' and that I should do it if it makes me happy. So he bought if for me."

The laugh comes bubbling out of Callan then, and I relax, feeling good that I made him happy, too. For weeks, I've been halfway in a daze of grief over Mama and Axel. It's nice to finally feel like I can smile again without bursting into tears. And the thing that gives me these little nuggets of happiness is making them happy. Well, that, and the little things they do to make me happy.

Callan brings me a fresh herb or a rabbit after a hunt. Ethan says I'm doing good even when I mix up the words for things he's shown me or forget to put soap in the laundry. Warrick said I should be happy, and he gave me three new experiences today—being queen of a motorcycle, going to a cold store, and getting food fast. And they all eat the food I make for dinner even when I burn it, or it tastes strange because I don't know what things go together.

"Let's get 'er done," Callan says. "How about right now?"

"Okay," I say, hopping up from the swing.

"This might get messy," he warns.

"Have you done it before?"

He throws his head back and laughs, then downs the rest of his beer and belches. "No, pet. This is *au naturale.*" He runs his hand dramatically through his shaggy brown hair.

"I think we can figure it out," I say. "Can you help?"

"Sure. Might as well get some more use out of these." He snags the gloves from where he dropped them at his feet on the porch, and we head inside. He opens the box and pulls out a big piece of paper. Staring intently at it, he mouths the words. At last, he points to the sink.

"Over there."

I like the way all these men tell me exactly what they want instead of making me guess things and get them wrong, like I did with Axel.

I go to the sink in the kitchen. Callan fishes a couple of plastic bottles from the box. He opens them and pours creamy white goo into the dark purple liquid. Shaking the bottle, he says, "Bend over the sink and let your hair hang into the basin.

I do as I'm told.

He gets behind me and squirts the goo into my hair, all over, until it's completely covered. "Now I'm going to massage this in, and then we wait for it to set."

I sniff the odd scent of the purple dye while Callan leans over my back and rubs his fingertips into my scalp until I want to purr. I remember Axel's fingers in my hair, doing the same thing with shampoo, and an ache pierces straight into my heart.

I gasp for breath, reeling with the sudden onslaught of pain that comes in bursts every time I remember something from our short time together.

Closing my eyes, I try to come back to the moment. This isn't Axel, who expected me to know everything and didn't tell me anything. It's Callan, who patiently answers the thousand little questions I have every day, and though sometimes he and the others laugh at me, they always let me know that it's okay if I don't know, that they're delighted by my lack of understanding. And then they teach me what I didn't know, so I can laugh with them.

"How you doin' down there?" Callan asks, his voice lower and gruffer than usual. I can feel something rigid pressed into my butt from the front of his hips, just like I felt from Axel when we were in the shower.

"Is that your cock?" I ask, remembering what Axel called it. I reach behind me to feel, and Callan lets out a groan.

I pull my hand back. "Did I do something wrong?"

"No, pet. You didn't do a thing except for being you," he says, easing back a little. "There. We're done."

I don't want to be done. Frustration rumbles in my throat as a growl. All these sensations and feelings are overwhelming, the way they come popping up like bubbles from the swamp, each one filled with something new—desire, confusion, grief, joy, pain—so many things every day that I don't know how to feel from one moment to the next. I hang my head in the sink for a moment, letting my sorrows drip down the drain with the droplets of color.

"So, show me what else you got," Callan says, fitting a plastic hat from the box over my head. He twists the dial on a small white thing on the counter, then we both head for the table.

One by one, I pull out the clothes Warrick purchased for me.

"Trust Warrick to make you look like a bag lady," Callan says, holding up an oversized T-shirt. "Of course he wouldn't want to show you off."

"Show me off?" I ask.

Callan drops the purple shirt he's holding onto the table. "If Ethan bought you clothes, we wouldn't be able to take you anywhere," he says. "Not without starting a riot."

"What's that?"

"A fight," he says.

"Why would Ethan pick clothes that would start a fight?"

His eyes make me feel warm and melty, like someone has reached inside my chest and rubbed my heart the way he massaged the goo into my scalp. "Because every guy in town would want to fuck you, plain and simple," he says. "Ethan and I vowed to protect you, so we'll happily tear out the throats of anyone who even makes eye contact with you. Got it?"

A shiver coils up my spine at his words, but I'm not afraid. While I don't want any more throat tearing, it feels like a full belly after a long hunt that the triplets vowed to protect me.

We finish going through the clothes, then pull out the hairbrush, the deodorant, the razors, the shampoo, and the tampons. Holding the box of tampons, I say, "Warrick didn't know how to use these. Do you?"

Callan's cheeks go bright red under his scruff. "Is that what he said?"

I nod, and he swallows, making the lump in his throat bob.

"I suppose I could show you," he says, his voice sounding choked.

A single ding vibrates in the air.

Callan rises from the chair at the table. "First, we get this dye off your chair. Come on back to the sink and lean over it."

He flips on the water, adjusts the water temperature, and trains it over my hair when I lean over the sink again. Purple water drains down the sink. When it turns mostly clear, he squirts some shampoo on my head and massages it into my scalp. His fingers are like magic, turning me into steamy heat, like dipping in the hot springs. Tingles of pleasure dance through my body, settling into the heat between my legs where Axel pierced me with his cock. But this feels only good, not painful. I sigh and push back against Callan.

His fingers still for a second, but then he pushes forward in response. The hot, rigid bulge of his cock pushes into my behind and sends a throb right into my center. I gasp and push back harder. Callan's breathing deep, too. Slowly, he begins to rhythmically rock his hips into me. Pleasurable sensations flood my body. I step my feet further apart, wishing he was between my legs like Warrick was on the bike today. I need more.

He flips off the water and rests one hand on the sink on either side of me, pushing me against the edge so hard it bites into my belly. He's breathing so hard I want to ask if he's okay, but my throat feels all trembly. Before I can gather my thoughts, his hands slide inside my t-shirt, up my sides, urging my arms up over my head. He tugs my shirt over my head, giving my hair a quick rub-down with the shirt to soak up some of the water. When I throw my hair back afterwards, it hits his shoulder, and he groans again.

"Ah, fuck, Luna," he murmurs, dipping his nose to the top of my head. His calloused hands run up and down my waistline, stroking his way to the front where he cups my breasts. His cock jerks against my backside, and he sucks in a breath.

The feel of his rough hands gliding across my soft skin fills me with confusing sensations. He pinches my nipples between his fingers, and a quick shock of need yanks tight inside me. Tingles and thrills pulse inside my lower belly. I close my eyes and fall into the pleasure coursing through my bloodstream. My mind goes all dream-like, like gazing at the water bugs as they skitter across the surface of the swamp, or when I'm belly up in my wolfskin in the hot sun.

Without a word, Callan pivots me around. I stand there, gripping the sink to stay upright, feeling dizzy suddenly. He didn't dry my hair well enough, and my dripping wet locks stick to my shoulders. Cool droplets stream down my face, neck, and torso. Callan is staring at me with eyes that make me want to melt into his arms.

"Oh fuck it," he says. "A man can only be so strong." He steps forward, grabbing me roughly and crushing his lips mine. I make a sound of surprise, but he swallows it whole. His slick tongue slides into my mouth, thrusting against mine. I'm too startled to move for a second. But then he reaches for my hand, lifting it and pulling it behind his neck. I raise the other one the same way, clinging to his shoulders while his tongue slides in and out against mine, and the thrilling sensations in my body increase until I'm ready to burst with excitement.

Suddenly, he wrenches his lips away.

"I can't..."

His forehead drops to mine, and we both breathe hard and heavy. The place between my legs still feels good, but now it aches, too.

"What happened?" I manage.

"That," Callan says. "Was a kiss." He reaches behind me, and his hand returns with the deodorant.

I lift my hands high, the way Warrick demonstrated. Callan gazes at me intently for a few seconds, slowly shaking his head while his nostrils flare. His tongue darts across his full lips, back and forth, like he's waiting for a juicy meal. He takes the top off the deodorant and pushes it up and down my armpits, one at a time.

"This is how you apply deodorant," he says, his voice a soft rumble.

I nod, unable to look away from his beautiful eyes. The creamy sensation of the deodorant stroking my skin feels lovely.

"After you shower, when we're heading into town, you can put this on," he says. "When you're around here, don't use it. I want to smell your natural essence. Your scent turns me on, Luna. I can smell you right now, how wet you are." He brushes his nose against mine. "It makes me fucking insane."

I reach for the shirt, meaning to dry myself more, but he catches my hand and presses it flat on the counter. "I want to smell you, not deodorant. But so-called civilized people like you to mask your scent."

"Why do they want me to mask my scent?" I say, my breath shallow against his cheek.

"So they don't get as turned on as I am right now." He lowers his lips to mine again, and his hands find my nipples.

Twirling and tweaking them sends shooting stars through my limbs, and the heat between my legs builds and aches with a starving kind of need. My lips part, and I'm panting now, unsure what to do with all the heat coursing through me but not wanting it to stop.

"Callan," I gasp. "I need—"

I don't know what I need. I feel a hurricane build inside me. When hurricanes came, Mama and I would hide, but this is the kind of storm that would make me race into the woods, dance naked in the wind, water and leaves plastering themselves to my body, throwing themselves against its indestructible power. That's what I feel inside as Callan's cock grinds into my belly. He slips a hand between my legs, where my pants are wet and hot. I moan, my head dropping back at the exquisite sensation of his fingers pressing against my swollen flesh.

"Oh, god, Luna… I'm about to…"

I don't know what he's about to do, but if it's the same thing pulsing through me, I'm about to do it, too. Suddenly, he yanks back. "Fuck," he says loudly, almost a yell.

"What?" I ask, torn between the pleasure and the fear that he's going to hurt me like Axel.

"I promised Ethan..." He points to the table. "Take that hairbrush and brush out your hair."

With that, he storms down the hall and into the bathroom, slamming the door behind him and leaving me confused and bewildered.

Chapter Eighteen

Luna

The triplets go off to a new job installing wires the next day after a quiet breakfast. I make dinner, but hardly anyone speaks through the meal. For some reason, I find myself thinking of this one time when I caught my foot in Virginia Creeper vines while a gator was eyeing me for its supper. Mama was having one of her funny feelings that day, so she was hiding in the house, sure that wolves were going to come for us. But we had to eat, so I went out anyway. I knew there were no wolves in the swamp, even if she didn't.

I shifted and raced into the woods, hoping for a lucky day and a fast catch. But then I got caught in the vines. I shifted back in a flash, used my fingers to free myself, and ran before the gator could grab me. That night, I headed home empty-handed to find Mama with a knife in her hand, ready to slit my throat because she thought I was one of the wolves, come to murder her.

Tonight feels almost as tense.

I cooked the swamp rabbits that were in Callan's traps today, but I just cooked it a little, leaving the meat nice and bloody. Still, the triplets are quiet, focused on eating, not even making conversation with one another.

"Did I cook the dinner wrong again?" I ask at last.

"It's great," Ethan says, wiping pink juice from his chin.

"Are you mad that I checked the traps without you?"

"It would be safer if you stayed with one of us when you go into the woods," Warrick says, scowling at me. "The Jacksonville pack doesn't take kindly to us using their hunting grounds."

"Besides, they might not like that you're living with us," Callan says.

"Why not?" I ask. "They didn't want me living with them. They can't pick where I do live."

Callan gives me a tight smile. "They might not like how it looks, you being Axel's former mate and all."

"How what looks?" I ask, glancing around in confusion.

"A pretty little lady like you, living with three ugly old dogs like us," Ethan says.

"What does it look like?" I ask. "Like you took me in and accepted me when they didn't?"

Warrick gives a rare grin, just one corner of his mouth pulling up. "That, too," he says with a chuckle.

"We'll show you where to hunt on your own, in case you get a hankering while we're out," Callan says, patting my hand. Then he pulls back real quick and casts a guilty look at Ethan. I remember what he said last night when he ran out of the kitchen, and I wonder what he promised his brother.

"I can take you out any time," Ethan says with a grin, covering my other hand with his. "I wouldn't mind seeing you shift."

Callan's foot shoots across the small space under the square table and clobbers Ethan's shin. Ethan curses and rubs at the bruise.

"Cut it out, you two," Warrick growls, and I feel that dominant energy pressing down on the table, forcing me to drop my gaze. The other two drop their heads and grumble.

There's more awkward silence.

"If it's not the dinner, or that I checked the traps alone, then is it my hair?" I guess, running my fingers through the beautiful purple strands, the color of spiderwort flowers. "Because even if you don't, I still love it, and I'm keeping it."

I peer up at Warrick from under my lashes, hoping he won't say otherwise because if he does, I think I'll have to change it back. He told me to do it, though, so I hope that's not it. Living with these men is so confusing. In the swamp, all I cared about was whether we had food to eat and if Mama was in a stable mood, which was seldom, or worked up, which was not. But even that is simple compared to trying to figure out what's wrong with the three grumpy, silent oafs sitting before me.

After dinner, Callan and Ethan start to clean the kitchen while Warrick disappears outside like he does whenever he's in a mood.

"Can I help?" I say, picking up my bowl and taking it to the sink.

"Nope," Callan says, plucking it from my hand and placing it in the sink.

The two men move around me like I'm a tree growing in the kitchen.

"I'm going out to have a beer on the front porch," I pronounce, the same way they usually do after dinner. "Come out if you want to join me."

No conversation ensues once I'm outside. Unlike most nights, they don't squabble or bicker, joke or play loud music. I wonder if it's because of what happened last night—whatever I did wrong that made Callan dash away to the shower like he was on fire. Maybe he told his brothers what I did wrong, and now they're all upset. Even though I don't *know* what I did, I know this new strangeness is because of me. When I arrived, everything was messy, but they were happy.

I brought this tension into their home. Worse, I don't understand how I did it or what to do about it.

I'm still thinking about it when I finish my beer and head inside, since no one came to join me. Callan is in the shower again. Since getting the showerhead fixed, these men are making up for lost time with the showers. I have to take one during the day when they're out because it seems like one of them is always in the shower lately.

I crawl into bed, and in the uneasy stillness of the typically raucous household, I close my eyes and will them to be happy again.

In the morning, I wake to the roar of motorcycle engines. I roll from the rumpled sheets, my heart hammering, afraid there will be another vampire fight. But when I run to the window, it's just Callan and Warrick on their bikes, ready to head off somewhere.

Callan's head swivels toward me, and for a second, our eyes lock. The same warm shivers I felt when he dyed my hair churn in my belly, but before I can even raise a hand to wave, they're gone in a cloud of dust and gravel.

My heart falters with the stinging ants of loneliness. A lump of emotion chokes my throat, blocking my breath. I pull on one of the new shirts Warrick bought me and pad to the kitchen on bare feet.

"Good morning," I say to Ethan, who sits at the table with a cup of coffee. I stop in the doorway to yawn and stretch my arms above my head. When I recover, Ethan's eyes are lingering on my body, and another fluttery feeling rolls through me.

"Morning, pup," he says in his growly before-breakfast voice.

"How's your neck healing up?"

"What? This?" He points to the stitched-up gash on his neck. "Nothing whiskey and painkillers won't cure."

I head to the cold box they call a fridge and snag a piece of rabbit sitting in last night's congealed sauce. I pluck the juicy meat out with my fingers and pop it in my mouth. Ethan watches my mouth with hunger evident in his gaze.

"You want some?" I ask, plucking up another piece and holding it up.

"Hell yeah, I want some of that." He angles his chair away from the table, extends one of his long legs, and pats his jeans-clad thigh. His torso is bare, as usual. "Bring that bowl of rabbit over here, and we'll eat it together."

"You're not mad at me anymore?"

"We weren't mad at you, pup." His lips roll between his teeth as he pats his thigh again. "It's just an adjustment, having a sexy little thing like you under the same roof as us."

I'm about to ask what that means, but when I reach the table, he grabs my hips, pivots me sideways, and pulls me onto his legs.

A yelp of surprise escapes my lips, but I melt a little when my arm connects with his warm skin.

He takes the bowl, sets it on the table, and picks up a morsel of rabbit. Instead of eating it, he holds it out for me. He pops the meat inside my mouth, leaving his fingers for a second so I have to curl my tongue around the meat and tug it free.

He lets out a little growl and then opens his mouth. I fish a piece from the bowl and slip it between his lips, my heart hammering hard for some reason. His teeth close around my fingers, and a wicked-looking smile appears.

"Oh!" I say in surprise, tugging at my hand. He seizes my wrist to hold it in place, and a look of mischief flashes on his face as he sucks on my fingers.

I close my eyes at the sensation of his hot, slippery tongue curling around my fingers. He lets out a low moan, and the vibration rolls through my fingers, up my arm, and down my body, settling in that achy pressure in my low belly. Something hard stirs under my bottom the same way it did when Callan was behind me. I slowly slide my finger free of Ethan's mouth and open my eyes. A smile curves my lips as I regard him. Maybe he won't run away like Callan did.

"Now that we're alone, I gotta ask," he says. "What did you and Callan do after I passed out the other night? Because whatever it was, it's got him all tied up in knots."

I like that he's thinking about the same thing as me. "He dyed my hair."

"Yeah? I like the purple. It's sexy. Makes you look less like a kid."

"I'm not a kid," I say, lifting my gaze toward a couple flies lazily circling the kitchen in the summer heat.. "I been taking care of myself since I was little, and my mama, too."

"I know," he says. "And you did a fine job of it. And now you look every inch the woman you are."

A surge of pleasure fills my heart, and I stroke my sleek hair.

"So," he says, shifting me on his lap so his cock is pushed right up against the softness of my bottom. "Then what did you do? You and Callan?"

Is this some kind of test? Am I going to get Callan in trouble? He said he'd promised something to Ethan. My lips part, but no words emerge.

"It's okay, you can tell me," Ethan says. His breathing quickens like he's hot on the trail of prey. My own breathing feels shallow, and I can't seem to think straight because it feels so good being near him like this.

"Well," I say, recalling the pleasure I felt when Callan kissed me. "He showed me how to use deodorant."

"Yeah?" He plucks out another piece of rabbit and feeds it to me. "Suck on my fingers."

I suck.

"Ah, fuck," he says, his eyes going back in his head. "And then what happened?"

A flush of heat ignites my cheeks and neck. "And then he kissed me—the way Axel did, not the way Mama did."

Ethan's eyes narrow as the hardness beneath my bottom pushes up like it's trying to escape being trapped between us. "Did he do anything else?"

I lift my hands to my breasts and touch each nipple through my shirt. "And then he touched me here."

He shifts his hips beneath me. "Did it feel good?"

"Yeah," I say, a little breathless.

"Did he show you how to use the other things Warrick bought you?" His voice sounds husky and strained.

I shake my head. "No. He left."

A few heartbeats of silence pass between us as Ethan studies me with a heated gaze.

"Get up," he says with a lift of his chin. "It's *my* turn."

"Your turn for what?" I ask, swallowing hard.

"You'll see," he says with a wicked grin, lifting me off his lap. My gaze lands on the significant bulge in his pants. He smirks when he catches me looking, then tugs at his jeans and stands. His fingers find the bulge, and he slowly strokes his fingers from the base to the top.

"See what you do to me?" he asks, a growl in his voice even as a teasing smile plays on his lips.

My pulse flutters in my throat, and I tear my eyes away to meet his gaze. "I did that?"

"Yes, Luna. You did that." He takes my hand and pulls me closer.

"Is that a good thing?"

"Want to feel?"

I nod mutely, letting him take my hand and press it to the thick ridge in his jeans. I curl my fingers around it as well as I can through the thick denim, staring down at it.

Suddenly, he pulls my hand away and drags me through the house to the bathroom. "Where's that bag of shit you got?" he asks.

I open the cabinet and pull out the sack with the stuff Warrick bought. Ethan rifles through it before pulling out the razors and shaving cream with a triumphant grin. "I'd better teach you to use these," he says. "Wouldn't want you to cut yourself, after all."

He crouches, retrieves the package the razor came in and rips it open. Running his thumb over the blade, he hisses when it slices his skin and a drop of blood appears.

"Oh, no," I cry. "Are you okay?"

He chuckles and sucks his thumb into his mouth.

"Does it hurt?" I ask. "What if you cut me, too?"

"Not a chance, pup," he says, pointing to the tub. "Take off your clothes and get in."

I slide the soft cotton from my torso as he turns on the hot water. Water streams from the spigot, but he doesn't pull out the metal device that makes it shoot out the showerhead. Instead, he inserts something in the drain, and water fills the tub.

His gaze rakes my entire body, and he groans like he's in pain.

"Are you okay?" I ask. "Is it your thumb?"

"Get in," he orders.

I step past him, brushing against his warm skin, and lower myself into the porcelain tub. Water crawls up my legs and hips, filling the basin. It's like the hot springs but without the trees and the birds and the smells of earth.

Razor and shaving cream in hand, Ethan climbs in opposite me, cranking off the water before settling into the tub.

I draw my legs up to my chest to make room for him.

"Leg, please." He extends his hand, and I stretch out one of my legs and rest it on his muscular thigh.

He pops the top off the shaving cream and presses a button, sending a bubble of white cream into his palm. With soft, sure strokes, he spreads it on my leg. His hands on my skin feel warm and good. Staring at me intently, the slightest smile curving his lips, Ethan draws the razor down my leg.

"See, no blood," he says, flashing me a grin and wiggling the razor at me. "It only makes you nice and smooth."

Suddenly, I remember Warrick saying I might want to be smooth between my legs for a real man, and that part of me burns hotter, making me squirm. Ethan watches me with a knowing smirk, then scoops water into his palm, rinsing my skin. He runs his palm up and down my calf. It feels so good I want to drop my head back and moan.

Ethan continues squirting the foamy white cream into his palm, spreading it over my skin and drawing the razor over it until my legs are hairless. His breath moves quickly from his heaving lungs, and I can see the big bulge of his cock still straining against his wet jeans.

When he's done with my calves, he parts my knees and moves closer to my body in the water, looking down between them. "Now comes the fun part," he says with a grin.

"What's the fun part?" I whisper.

"Your pussy," he growls in a voice so deep I barely recognize it.

"My what?"

"Spread your legs and rest them on my thighs and scoot closer." His tongue darts across his lips.

Swirls of tingly feelings shoot through my lower belly as I do as I'm told. Water no longer touches the place between my legs that feels so good and aches so bad.

He squirts another cloud of shaving cream in his hand and touches it between my legs. I gasp with pleasure, my hips rising on their own. Ethan moans and spreads the cream into my hair, massaging me until I'm whimpering like my wolf when she's injured. He just chuckles and holds up the razor, slowly stroking it down the side of my hair. He works slowly, and each stroke is torture. Not because he's cutting me or making me bleed, but because I want his touch again, and when I get a bit of it, it's not enough.

"You like that, pup?" he asks, though the shine in his eyes and the upward slant of his mouth says he knows the answer already.

"Yes," I say, my voice somewhere between a whisper and a moan.

He chuckles and spreads open the outer layer of my heat, gazing down at the secret within like he's never seen something so wondrous. I raise my hips slowly, and he slides a finger across the swollen bud between those lips. I give a little mewling cry.

"Goddamn, Luna," he growls. "I want to fuck you so hard your head explodes."

"What?" I ask, drawing away slightly. "Don't do that!"

Ethan only grins and shakes his head, laying a hand on my knee and pulling me back again. "Don't worry, pup. I won't. Now let me finish before *I* explode."

Don't trust the wolves.

Mama's last words echo through my mind, but they seem far away now. I squeeze my eyes shut and hold my breath, feeling each scrape and drag of the sharp metal against my skin. My breath comes in little pants as the swirling in my belly increases. The soft clatter of plastic against porcelain and the small thwack of metal on the rim of the tub lets me know Ethan's set the razor and shaving cream to the side.

I lay still, barely breathing, my heart feather light as it tiptoes in my chest. I have the same ache I had with Callan in the kitchen, the one I had in the shower with Axel before he tasted me and made the world open before me. I don't know what to do with all this feeling, but I know I don't want Ethan to leave like Callan did, and I don't want him to hurt me like Axel did.

"Want to feel?" Ethan asks, one of his fingers stroking up and down my newly bare skin.

My eyes flutter open, meeting his intense gaze. I bite my lip and give a slight nod. He takes my hand and lowers it between my legs. It feels so smooth that I let out a little sigh of pleasure, exploring the soft, silky skin he touched. For a minute, Ethan only watches, his breath coming in quick little huffs when I move inside the outer layer, like he did. With a growl, he knocks my hand aside and pushes one of his thick fingers inside my slick hole.

I let out a cry of surprise and pleasure even though there's a pinch of pain inside me, too.

He lets out a guttural groan, his eyes going back in his head. "Holy High Priestess," he says, his voice a moan of anguish. "You're so fucking tight."

"Are you okay?" I ask, trying to clear my head.

His gaze snaps to mine, and he grins. "Oh, pup, I'm more than okay," he says, slowly drawing his finger out and pushing it back in even deeper. "A tight pussy is a very good thing."

I moan, my thighs quaking as his finger slides in and out again and again.

"You like that, little pup?" he croons.

"Yes," I breathe.

His thumb makes little circles around the swollen bud, and my whole body arches this time. "I'm going to try to get another finger in there," he says, his voice rough. "Stretch you out a little, in case you ever want one of our cocks inside you. You want that, Luna? You want one of our cocks inside this tight little hole?"

"Yes," I moan, feeling a delicious stretch that's almost painful as he works another finger inside me. My walls clench tight around them.

He groans and closes his eyes, his nostrils flaring as he takes a few deep breaths. "Does that hurt?" he asks.

"A little," I admit.

"Did Axel put his cock inside you?"

"For a minute," I say, hoping he'll stop talking about Axel. I don't want that to happen again—the pleasure to be replaced by pain, and the searing burn on my arm, and the feeling like my wolf was ripped out of my body and devoured by his.

But my wolf is only happy inside me, urging me on in a playful way that doesn't scare me. When I relax, Ethan starts to slide his fingers in and out again, the way Axel's cock did. This doesn't feel like Axel, though. There's no pain after he starts moving, and he's circling his thumb around the place that makes me feel like my head really might explode. His eyes are clouded and halfway closed, his lips slightly parted as he watches his fingers pump into me. His gaze is soft and warm, though, with no determination or command like Axel's.

I close my eyes and let myself trust him. The desperate sensations inside me builds, and my hips rise and fall on their own, seeking some kind of relief I can't find, the kind that Axel gave me with his mouth. I've never felt so good as that moment, better than a hot summer day lazing I the sun or watching dragonflies dart around the cattails, better than howling at the full moon in autumn, or racing through the fallen leaves at a gallop.

"Ethan," I gasp, grasping the edge of the tub as I feel something about to break inside me.

"Yeah, puppy?" His smile fills my chest with joy, and he increases the pressure and slows his thumb, dragging it across my slippery nub. "What do you want?"

"I want—" I can't answer, though. Words escape me as pleasure explodes through my body, releasing the tension and need aching inside me. My vision blurs, and my head drops back as my hips rise, my knees opening wide as I cry out in helpless bliss. An overwhelming stream of color and sensation flows through my body, my mind. It's stunning, and there's no painful burn in my arm, no confusion in my soul. I am home, and I never want it to end.

Chapter Nineteen

Ethan

I've fucked hundreds of women, but shaving Luna's pussy is the most truly erotic moment I've ever experienced. When she orgasmed, she looked fucking transcendent. I'd never admit it, but I'm shaken by the intensity of what happened. Hell, I couldn't explain it if I tried, how fingering her pussy made me feel things that fucking twenty women couldn't.

I'm not the man with the words, so afterwards, we lie in silence on her bed, with her cuddled in the crook of my arm. For once, I'm not thinking about when I can get up and go, or even whether it's time for a sandwich. Having her body next to mine feels fucking fantastic. It scares the hell out of me, but I don't want to stop. This feels too good to fuck it up by fucking her. And that scares me even more. Since when do I not want to fuck a gorgeous, willing woman?

Since never, that's when. The fact that my cock definitely feels different about that reassures me that I'm not turning into a pussy. I've had the world's longest, hardest hard-on for an hour straight, and every time I think about the stranglehold of her hot, wet cunt on my fingers, I just about come my pants like a teenager.

Her breathing is deep, and I think she's fallen asleep until she speaks. "Tell me a story," she says, her voice edged with sleepiness.

"A story?" I ask, trying not to sound incredulous. "I'm not the bedtime story type of guy."

"Good thing it's not bedtime," she says, squirming onto her back in my arms. "Tell me what it was like growing up out here, away from the swamp."

I push her long, purple hair away from her face. "Where's this coming from?"

"I don't know," she says. "I want to know more about you— all of you boys."

I sigh and roll onto my back, my arm still pillowing her head. "That's not something I do, pup. Think about the past. That shit is dead and gone."

"Then it'll be easy to talk about." Her lips curve in the sweetest smile, one that blow-torches my walls into ash.

I continue to finger strands of her silken hair, steeling myself to dredge up memories of our childhood. Any other woman asked me this, I'd tell her to fuck off and mind her business. But Luna's not any woman. "What do you want to know, pup?"

"Whatever you see fit to share," she says. Her head nestles into my chest, and I swear I've died and gone to the place in the sky that men like me don't ever go.

"Well, our daddy was a real son of a bitch. How's that?"

She curls her small fingers into my little patch of chest hairs and tugs. "More."

"Ouch," I say, laughing and grabbing her hand. "I'm already injured, and I might die of blue balls this very night. I don't need my chest hairs pulled out, too."

"I'm sorry," she coos, stroking her small hand over my pecs. "What's blue balls?"

"Never you mind, pup," I say. "But keep plucking my nipple like that and you're going to find out how it feels when I empty them."

"Oh!" she says, pulling her hand away, her cheeks turning a shade of pink that makes me want to simultaneously wrap her up in a protective hug and fuck her pretty little mouth until tears run down her cheeks from gagging on my cock until she can't breathe. My head is so fucking confused, I don't know what's what.

She lays her gentle hand on the center of my chest. "Is this okay?"

God, my fucking chest aches with her sweetness. "Yeah," I say, covering her hand with mine. "It's more than okay."

"Will you tell me?" she asks. "I've told all y'all about life in the swamp with Mama."

I take a few seconds to conjure up something to say about dear old dad. It's the last thing I want to talk about, but pleasing her wins out over not wanting to rehash this old shit. "He really was a rotten son of a bitch," I say after a minute. "Mean as a snake. He fixed rich people's pools and did upkeep on them... Same kind of thing we do, but more steady, less odd jobs. According to his drunk ass, it was all our fault that he wasn't living in one of them fancy houses with a pool."

"Why?"

I shrug and caress her silky skin to keep myself busy while I get this out of the way. "He got meaner the deeper into goblin juice he got. We all had our way of dealing with him. Warrick, he got real quiet, same way he does now when he's simmering on something. Callan always tried to be the perfect son to keep him from having something to go after us for, picking up our room and helping our mama and shit like that. And me…" I let out a bitter chuckle. "I tried to lighten the mood, maybe tell a joke and get him laughing."

"Why'd you need to joke?" she says, tracing circles along my belly that have my cock dancing in the wet jeans I'm still wearing after our bath.

"Dad was always pissed when he came home drunk because he couldn't find goblin blood and tried to kill the craving with booze. Those times were the worst." My forehead furrows, and a few emotional rocks land on my chest as I imagine Dad's foul temper. "I learned early there was one way to cool his temper, and that was to get him laughing. Otherwise, he'd take out his anger on us with a two-by-four—that'+-s a piece of wood, in case you wondered. It was best to get him laughing before that happened."

My whole body tenses with the memory, and I stop moving my hand against her arm. Skipping down memory lane is twisting my insides into knots.

"Ethan," she says, her voice choked. "That sounds awful."

"That's why I hate talking about this shit," I say. "But don't go feeling sorry for me. It was nothing compared to what you went through out there with just your mama. And it wasn't all bad. I felt real proud when I could get Dad to laugh before he walloped us. I protected all four of us if I got him laughing. That's when I knew I did good, that we'd all be alright. Warrick and Mama and Callan all looked at me like I was their fuckin' savior, I tell you. That's about the best feeling in the world."

The distant whine and snarl of motorcycle engines drifts through the open window.

"Shit, Luna. Get up and get dressed. We've got five minutes, tops."

She scrambles from the bed. "Why? What's happening?"

"My brothers are happening." Shame nooses my insides at taking advantage of Luna.

"Callan said he promised you," she says, pulling on a new shirt from the pile Warrick bought her. "What did he promise?"

"You can't tell anyone what we did today, got it?" I say, rolling out of bed and dragging off my wet jeans. My brothers would fucking murder me if they knew I'd been fingering up our little pet, the one who's off limits to all of us.

Luna digs through the bag of clothes and pulls out pair of shorts. "Why do we have to keep everything a secret?"

"Because people tend to get jealous when everyone wants to fuck the same girl, and only one person does it."

"What's fuck?" she says.

"What we just did in the tub," I say, throwing my long hair back and yanking on a fresh pair of jeans. "That's finger-fucking."

She nods, looking thoughtful and going way too fucking slow with dressing. Obviously she doesn't get the urgency of the situation.

"What's jealous?" she says, grabbing her hairbrush and brushing out her long tresses.

"Competitive. They want what you want, and they might fight you for it."

More like tear out my stitches and leave me to bleed out.

"Like when the gators fight over fresh kill?"

"Exactly like that," I say.

The motorcycles are getting closer, and we need to get out of the bedroom.

"Come on," I say, grabbing her shoulders, pivoting her around, and urging her out of the bedroom. "You get into the kitchen, and I'll put some music on in the front room. Pretend we've just been here learning more manners today."

"What kind of manners? What should I say?" she says, trotting after me.

I rush into the living room and pick up a *Pixie Dust* album from Callan's record collection. I fit it on the turntable and move the arm to gently place the needle on the vinyl. "Just say you learned how to act civilized in town. Don't call it manners."

Heavy metal blasts through the speakers, filling the room. I pull her close for a last quick embrace. "I promise, Luna," I murmur into her hair. "If you keep this a secret, next time we're alone, I'll make you feel as good as you felt in the tub today. Deal?"

I release her as Warrick and Callan power up the driveway and park their beasts.

"Deal," she says with a sexy little smile that makes my cock hard all over again and leaves me wondering if I've just made a deal with the devil. But, damn, if I have to piss off my brothers to get some more of Luna's sweet little pussy, that's a risk I'm willing to take. Now that I've gotten a glimpse of her pleasure, nothing can stop me from going back for more.

Chapter Twenty

Luna

I hurry around the kitchen trying to get something together that looks like I was making dinner before Callan and Warrick got home. They tromp into the house in their heavy work boots and grab beers from the fridge. My spine is stiff as I throw some wild lettuce and meat in a frying pan. I don't like keeping things from them, but I don't want Ethan to get in trouble, and I definitely want more of whatever he gave me today in the tub.

Callan and Warrick plunk their beers down on the table, the legs of their chairs scraping the floor as they drag them back and drop into them. Ethan strolls in like there's not a secret in the world, grabs a beer, and joins them at the table.

"Would you look at us," he says, popping the tab on his beer so it lets out a hiss. "Taking a load off while a fine woman makes us dinner. Never thought I'd see the day."

"I've made dinner before," I say.

"I feel downright domesticated," Warrick says. I catch him watching me funny, and I quickly turn my back.

"What'd you get up to today, Luna?" Callan asks. He sounds casual, not mad, so that's good.

"Just learning some manners," I say, then remember Ethan said not to tell them that. This whole lying business is going to take practice. A tendril of smoke curls up from the pan, and I cuss, realizing I forgot to put in oil before the other stuff. I scrape frantically to get the lettuce off the bottom of the pan and throw a scoop of bacon grease under it.

When I turn away from the stove, Ethan is laughing silently. I glare at him.

Callan has his head raised, sniffing the air. Maybe he doesn't like the burning smell.

"What kind of manners?" he says at last, sharing a look with Warrick that makes my heart jump.

"You know... Stuff to make me act civilized in town."

"That's good," he says. "Learning how to co-mingle in society can't hurt."

"Uh-huh," I say.

"You're burning the meat," Warrick says.

I spin back around. "Shit!"

They're all laughing now, and I'm fuming mad but also grateful that things aren't as tense as they were this morning. But by the time I'm done cooking, the air over the table is silent and brittle as a sun-bleached bird's nest, a delicate twig that will snap at any moment. Ethan keeps his head down and doesn't talk or joke around like usual or bicker with Callan. Warrick is silent and frowning, but he doesn't press us down with what Callan explained is his wolf's dominance. He doesn't have to dominate us tonight. We are all subdued already.

I don't want to sit on the porch alone again tonight, hoping one of them will join me, so I go to the bedroom across from Warrick's. I sit on the bed, all my good feelings from earlier gone. This isn't my room. It's Ethan and Callan's room, and because of me, they're both sleeping on the floor in the other room. Only Warrick and I have rooms. If I was gone, they could have their bed back, and they wouldn't be mad at each other every day.

I'm the cause of this mess. I don't know how they know, but I'm sure they do. They know what Ethan did to me, and they don't like it. Maybe they don't want me to feel good or have some fun, as Warrick said, after all. Just like Axel, they say this is my home and that they'll protect me, but in the end, if I don't do it the way they want, then they don't want me around.

I turn off the light and try to sleep. The full moon is just rising, and my wolf is restless inside me, wanting to run and hunt. I toss and turn, sweating in the sultry night. Even when I strip off my clothes and throw off the sheet, it's too hot, and I can't make my thoughts be quiet and go to sleep so that my body can follow. The moon rises up my window until I can barely see it, and I'm halfway asleep when the yelling starts.

"What the fuck, Ethan?" Callan roars, dragging me from my frustrating attempt at sleep.

"I don't know what you're talking about," Ethan yells back. "Get off me!"

I hold my breath, tensed and listening.

"You fucked her, didn't you?" Callan yells. "You fucking asshole, you can't keep your dick in your pants for two fucking weeks?"

"I didn't fuck her," Ethan hollers back. "Want to check my dick?"

There's a thud, and I jump up and tiptoe to the door to listen.

"She came," Callan growls. "I can smell it on her."

Scuffling noises follow. "Maybe she pleasured herself," Ethan says, sounding out of breath and strained. "Chicks do that, you know."

Callan sounds more pissed. "We had a deal, *brother*, or does a pact between brothers mean nothing to you when there's pussy involved?"

"You broke it first!" Ethan yells back.

I look down, sliding a hand between my legs to feel the smooth skin Ethan touched earlier. "This is your fault, then," I whisper.

As I suspected, their fight *is* about me. Tears prick the corners of my eyes. I never wanted to make anyone angry or upset. I thought I could be one of them since they were so accepting of me. They never make me use silverware when my hands are better, never bind my soul to theirs and then rip it out with barely a warning. They're good to me, and I want to be good to them. Bringing anger and fights to their house is not being good to them.

Warrick chimes in at last. "Cut this shit out," he growls, and the other two fall silent. "This is just what I didn't want to fucking happen, but you two dicks-for-brains swore there'd be no conflict. Now look at the pair of you, sneaking around trying to get it any way it comes. That little whisp of ass couldn't withstand one good pounding from any of us."

I can feel the shame all the way from here, the way Warrick's wolf dominance makes me hang my head the same as his brothers.

He sighs. "You can't live under the same roof with a woman like that and expect anything else."

A woman like me. What does that mean? I don't even know what kind of woman I am, so how can he know?

"This stops right now," Warrick growls when no one answers him. "We're *brothers*. We walk to the depths of hell to protect each other. Nothing and no one comes between us. Have I made myself clear?"

Silence so fragile it could shatter shrouds the front room.

Once again, it's come down to this—it's *my* presence that stirs conflict. I know what I have to do. Tears track down my cheeks as I pad to the back door on silent, bare feet. I can hear

Ethan accusing Callan of "doing it first" again as I ease open the screen door and slip outside. I don't let the screen door thwack shut. I guide it closed, so it doesn't make a sound.

Outside, I take a shaky breath and sink to the ground, ignoring the mosquitoes that swarm in for a taste of my blood. It's been a month since I shifted, a month that I've been here. A month to learn human manners and grow to love these big, stubborn, strong, grumpy men. But now it's time to leave them.

I shift into my wolf form, relieved that the pain in my chest dulls when I'm a wolf. Wolves love, but they don't feel the other complicated emotions humans do. Things are simpler this way. The moon guides me as I shift and run. I race for the creek that splits the property and wade into the knee-deep water. Then, I head downstream so they won't be able to track my scent. When I've gone far enough, I scramble onto the opposite bank and run.

I don't think about where I'm going. My wolf knows where home is. She leads me to Bogbeast Waters, the full moon lighting our way.

The glowing orb is lowering toward the horizon, and the first birds of morning have begun to call by the time I reach our old place. I scent my way there, pulling myself from the water and onto the dry land and shaking off. Even with my wolf eyes I can tell something is wrong. Our tiny house, the one I built when I was turning from a child to a woman and patched a hundred times… It's gone.

I know I'm in the right place. My nose wouldn't lie, and even if it did, I can see the remnants of our home scattered around our little island. Twisted tin and splintered wood poke up from the ground. The scent of molding cloth under the pile tells me they didn't take anything. They just tore it all down, destroyed the only home I have left.

Pain strikes through my wolf heart, and I tip back my head and howl. It's a mournful howl encompassing everything I've lost, from Mama to Axel to the triplets to my home, my heart, my roots.

An answering howl issues forth from the woods to my right, startling me back to reality.

I crouch, ready to slink in the opposite direction and fade into the night. The last thing I expected was another wolf out here in the Waters, risking gators and ogres and bog beasts.

I lift my nose, scenting the air and catching something familiar. Did one of the triplets follow me without my noticing?

Suddenly, a large wolf leaps onto my island and shakes, water spraying from his pelt. I bare my teeth, growling as my hackles rise. I'll fight to the death to protect this tiny hillock of land, all I have left, even if there's nothing else left of my home.

The wolf shifts with majestic grace, and Axel stands before me in all his naked glory.

My wolf cowers to her belly, a low whine escaping my throat as pain spirals into my chest. I never thought I'd see him again, never wanted to. Seeing him, it all rushes back—the wonderful part before the mating, the painful mating, the bond and the breaking, and worst of all, watching Mama die after everything. When it all bursts to the surface like a gator snatching prey, I want to die all over again.

"Easy, Luna," Axel says, palms outstretched.

I throw back my head and howl again, this time for the echoes of the True Mate bond that linger in my bones. I want him out of me forever, but he's still in there, clinging to my bones.

He seems to know what this plaintive cry means, or maybe he feels it, too. He sways on his feet, then goes to his knees in front of me so he's on my level.

"Luna, stop," he says in a choked voice. "I came to make amends, and when I saw your house had been torn apart… I've been out here every night looking for you, hoping that I could warn you if you came back. Whoever was here… They might be hunting you. You're in danger, Luna. You need to come with me. Come back to the pack. We can protect you."

I back away from him, snarling.

"I understand you hate me. I don't blame you. What I did to you…" Axel shakes his head. "What I did to you was as painful for me as it was for you. So I know how much I hurt you."

More low growls rumble in my throat. He can't begin to know the pain I've felt. It's not possible. He would die. A loud splash comes from the nearby swamp, but my eyes remain glued to Axel's.

"You have every right to be angry," he says, still holding out a hand. I could bite that hand off, and he knows if. But he's letting me know he trusts me, even if I can't do the same. "I made a mistake. I realize that now. But your life is in danger, and that's more important than my pride—or yours. Come with me."

Callan explained wolf dominance to me, how a stronger wolf can enforce their will the way Warrick does. He uses it to keep order in his household. I've felt it many times since moving in. But Axel has never commanded me that way, never forced his will on me. I could feel he had it, but he never made me behave, even when I was acting wild in front of the pack. And even now, as I tense, waiting for the push of his wolf's dominance, I feel only his pleading eyes on me. After a long moment, he shifts back into his wolf. The sight of it sends another spear of agony through my wolf's heart. She loves this wolf.

He gives me one last searing gaze, then turns and pads away. When he reaches the edge of my tiny island, he stops and pivots his head to look at me. His wolf eyes catch the moonlight and reflect the calming silvery glow at me. He won't force me to go. He's showing me that. This is my choice.

I stand pinned to the boggy marsh ground, caught in a web of indecision and regret, past hurts and future fears. I tear my gaze from his and back to my destroyed home. Another splash erupts from the swamp, only it's closer now. There's nothing for me here, no safety. I'll be exposed, food for gators and swamp monsters.

I turn back to Axel.

Come.

I startle at the clarity of his intention, as if I heard him speak aloud. But he's still not using his dominance to force me. I can be stubborn and stay here to be attacked, or I can go with him, to a pack that's already cast me out and done worse than attack me. All I have is his word, and I know how little that counts.

There's no chance of survival out here by myself, though. I no longer want to die. No matter how sad I am about leaving the triplets' house, it didn't crush me the way Mama's death did. There is still reason to live.

And there's a chance that can happen with Axel. So, when he turns away and bounds onto the next hillock, I hesitate for only a moment more, and then I follow.

Chapter Twenty-One

Luna

The familiar sight of Axel's house sends another shock of pain through me. I wonder when the waves of hurt will stop crashing over me, taking me by surprise. On his porch, Axel shifts back to a man. He seemed so big when I first saw him, but after a month with the triplets, he no longer looks like a giant. He's strong and muscular and tall, but he's also lean and tight where they are bulging walls of muscle.

I stay in my wolf form. I don't trust him—or myself. My wolf soul still cries for him to be ours, even after what he did.

He sighs and opens the door, gesturing for me to enter. I pad inside and scent the floor and the air. His house is so much cleaner than the triplets,' even now that we clean it every few days. But I prefer the smell of dirt and forest that we track into the dirty cabin over the clean, old smell of Axel's house. I also don't care for the scent of Ama that lingers.

"It's late," Axel says with a sigh. "You can make yourself comfortable in the guest room. Unless…"

He gives me a searching look, then shakes his head and turns, heading up the stairs without waiting for an answer. I pad after him on my wolf paws. He swings open the door to one of the bedrooms and gestures for me to enter.

"You're safe here, Luna," he says quietly. "No one will bother you. That includes me."

He waits, like he expects me to answer. When I don't, he turns and trudges off down the hall to his room, the room where—

I block the thought before it can get started. This house is haunted with memories that are worse than ghosts. I know my human can't handle them tonight, that my wolf has to take care of her. I hop onto the bed and curl up at the foot, still in my wolfskin, and fall asleep.

That's my first night at Axel's house. The next day, he goes to work before I wake and comes home at dark looking tired. We eat dinner in silence. He watches me, but he doesn't mention the True Mate bond again. The second night, he gives me a toothbrush and stands in the bathroom door while I brush. He asks if I'm going to sleep in the guest room. There's something he's not saying, but I don't know what. I think he's afraid I'll run again. He doesn't know what happened in the month we were apart, but he must know I have nowhere else to go.

I tell him yes, and I go to bed. I lie awake, turned to the window where the past-full moon shines through the thin white curtains. Are the guys out on their porch, drinking beer right now? Did they forgive Ethan for what we did? Is everything back to good between them now that I'm gone? I hope I did the right thing, that they're happy and getting along again. I smile and close my eyes, wondering how it's possible to feel happy and sad at the same time.

The next day is the same. I wander around Axel's small house, wondering what to do with myself. The house is clean, so I can't help him there. I'm under strict instructions not to leave the house while he's gone, so I can't go wander and look for edible plants like I could outside the triplets' house. And when I think about making food, I remember the way the pack looked at me when I ate in front of them. I shudder and decide not to even attempt to cook.

Axel hasn't commented on my hair even though I came out of my wolfskin on my first day here. He gives me clothes to wear that are too small for him—stretchy little pants, a tight shirt that barely covers my nipples, a very small skirt, and other random items he has on hand.

That night, he comes to the door of my bedroom when I'm getting under the blankets. It's raining outside, fat droplets slapping the windows and making the screens bow in and out. Axel stands there watching me, an expression on his face that I can't read. But I can feel sadness sitting heavy around him like a dense fog over the water that doesn't lift even when the sun shines.

"Goodnight," I say, not sure what to say to this quiet man. He's not grumpy like Mama or Warrick, where you can feel something brewing under the mood. He's weighed down by his own sadness, one that goes far deeper than any mood. If he's sad about me, it's his own doing.

He sighs and runs a hand through his hair, then steps into the room. His lips are tight, and he pauses, like he might turn and leave. Instead, he comes to the bed and sits down on the edge. Lightning flashes outside, and thunder makes me wince.

I wonder if the water will rise up to claim what remains of the little house I built so long ago.

"Luna," Axel starts, clearing his throat before going on. "I want you to know, I'm sorry. I'm—I'm just so fucking sorry."

He looks at me with pleading, miserable eyes.

I know what I'm supposed to say. I snuggle down under the blankets, a shiver going through me when the wind brings a fine mist of rain through the window. "I forgive you."

He pulls back, surprise making his brows lift. "You do?"

"Yes," I say. "You were right. We don't belong together."

"That's not... Luna, I'm sorry because I was *wrong.*"

"Maybe you were wrong when you did it," I agree. "We were meant to be together then. You said we weren't, but my wolf always knows. But by doing what you did, you made your words come true."

His blue eyes search mine for a long minute. "Is that really how you feel?"

I nod, feeling as sad as he looks to admit this truth. "Because you separated us, we're no longer meant to be together. Fate wouldn't mean for me to be with someone who would hurt me that way. I didn't understand then, but I do now."

"Your wolf doesn't feel anything?"

My wolf feels lots of things. She's crying inside me, even as my human eyes remain dry. I know that I'm right. We can never be meant to be together after what he did. That was the whole point. And it worked. Being here now, I see how wrong we are, no matter how much my wolf longs to bond with him again, to crawl into his warm arms and let him hold us tight through the storm, put back together all the parts that were ripped away by severing the bond.

That's not possible, though. It's like unbreathing a breath you already took.

"You severed the bond between us," I say, my fingertips absently stroking the crescent moon scar on my arm. "It's not there anymore, no matter how much you regret it."

Without another word, Axel rises and leaves the room, closing the door quietly behind him. A long roll of thunder barrels toward us, so loud it rattles the house when it passes. I curl onto my side, my chest aching with loneliness.

When I wake, the sun shines in the window, beating down on my face and arms as it makes its morning ascent in the sky. I stumble out of bed, get ready for the day, and then head downstairs. The very air in the house feels heavy and sad. I grab a piece of bread and look for things to put inside it. Ethan taught me about sandwiches. The thought of him makes me smile as I layer on a cock-like piece of meat, some tiny orange slices floating in their juices, and some salty green fruits with a little red center in each one. I wrap it all up and take it onto the porch to eat, knowing by the sweet juice already running down my wrist that it'll be a messy one.

I sit on the steps and take a bite, trying to decide what to do. I don't know where I belong, but it sure isn't here. I can't go back to the brothers and destroy their peace, and I can't go home to the swamp. If there's anything left in the debris of our house, it's probably not useable, and I don't know how to get more tin and nails.

A motorcycle rounds the corner and captures my attention. My heart leaps in my chest and then races as if to greet the rider. Water sprays from beneath the tires as it speeds in my direction. I squint at it as it approaches, my frozen heart beginning to thaw. I can't let myself hope, and yet, I do.

There can only be one man riding with no shirt, hair flying back, and the tattoo of a wolf family on his broad chest.

Callan.

I want to leap up and run to him, throw myself into his arms. But then I remember leaving, and why I left. Has he come to warn Axel about the conflict I'll bring?

My wolf woofs happily inside me, insisting he's come for a different reason, that he's come for *us*.

Callan rolls right up the sidewalk and parks in the sparse grass in front of Axel's home. He kicks the stand down and swings his long leg over the frame of the bike.

"How'd you find me?" I say, folding my arms over my chest and trying to hide my smile as he stalks over.

"I'm a wolf." His arms cross, too, as he faces me, studying me with a somber expression. "I scented until I found you."

"Really?" I ask, uncrossing my arms when my sandwich dribbles juice down my leg. I shove it in my mouth, so I won't say something else, like begging him to take me back and promising I won't do any more shaving with Ethan, no matter how good it feels.

"Come home, Luna."

I swallow down the sandwich even though it sticks in my aching throat. "I don't have a home."

"You're wrong," he says. "You left before we could tell you."

"You were fighting," I say, my eyes aching as hard as my throat. "I made you fight."

He scratches his beard. "We're a bunch of stubborn men," he says. "We find things to fight about whether you're there or not. But you know what happens then?"

I shake my head.

"We work things out," he says. "If you stuck around, you'd have known that. We came to a decision. Warrick, too. We all agree, your home is with us—if that's where you want to be."

I nod, a tear leaking down my cheek.

Callan lets his arms fall by his side. "I saw your shack. It's been destroyed."

"I know," I whisper.

Footsteps storm through the house, heading for the front door. Instinctively, my arms squeeze tighter on my chest, and I back away from Callan. Callan may have worked things out with his brothers, but now I'm causing a fight between him and Axel.

"You're trespassing," Axel roars as the screen door swings open, banging against the wall. "You have two minutes to get your mangy ass off my property before the whole pack arrives and tears every organ from your ugly corpse." His hair's all wet like he just got out of the shower, and he's shirtless like Callan.

His muscles are taught, water droplets clinging to his shoulders, and I can't help but gulp when I gaze at his beautiful form, his smooth golden skin and the small tattoos on his shoulders and forearm. But then I turn to Callan, his own muscles bunched with rippling power, his skin inked and scarred in a dozen places. He's just... *More*. Bigger, wilder, stronger; with more tattoos, more scars, more hair, more beard. And there's three of him and only one of Axel.

"Oh, yeah?" Callan asks, puffing his chest up even bigger. "You think I'm scared of the kind of dumbass who would sever a True Mate bond with this sweet little lady?"

Axel's eyes narrow, and for the first time, I feel the edge of his dominance shimmering in the air between us like heat rising off the still pools of water on the most scorching summer days. The intensity of it makes me shiver and gasp, even though I can feel that it's only beginning.

"Get off my property, mutt," he says to Callan. "She's mine."

He steps forward, resting a gentle hand on the back of my neck, and a wave of soothing comfort washes over me. I stare up at him, my mouth dropping open. He has some kind of... Magic. That's the only way to describe how he can calm me with a single touch of his hand, how I can know instantly that he means me no harm. My wolf settles inside me, content.

But it's not right. He *hurt* us. I'm not safe here, and his magic only makes me more sure of it. I duck away from him, and before he can touch me again, Callan is up in his face.

"Sorry, dude. You gave up your rights to her. She belongs with us now." Callan circles Axel like he's getting ready to attack.

Axel doesn't back down. Instead, he circles to face Callan as the bigger man moves around him. "Abunch of outlaw punks?" Axel asks, spitting the words at his enemy with a scoff. "No way does she belong with the likes of *you.*"

"You had your chance with her," Callan retorts with a shrug. "Not our fault you threw her out. She was a lone, banished wolf when we found her. She wasn't on pack land. By every werewolf law, she's fair game. And what tasty game she is..."

"You motherfucking mongrel," Axel snarls, leaping for Callan.

I jump forward before he can hit my savior. I wedge myself between them, slamming my palms on their chests as hard as I can. Startled, they each take a step back and stare at me.

"Please stop!" I yell, stomping my foot. "I'm tired of all you males making decisions for me."

They both blink at me, and then they both start talking at once. I hold up a hand and bark at them to listen to what I have to say for once.

First, I turn to Axel. "You willfully severed our bond," I remind him. "You told me I had to leave the pack. Callan and his brothers found me in the swamp, ready to die. They *saved* me."

Axel's Adam's apple—Callan explained that one to me—bobs up and down as he digests my words.

"Like I said," Callan starts, but I send him a glare that silences him.

"They took care of me," I say, turning back to Axel. "Not you. You rejected me, and not just me, but my wolf. You didn't want me as a mate, the other half of your soul. You can't just tell me to come back like it didn't happen. It happened. Our bond is *gone*." I point to the dull scar on my arm, the one that no longer glows with the power of the moon and our bond. "No matter how sorry you are, it will never return."

I swipe angrily at a tear, and Axel reaches for me. "Luna, I…"

I bat his hand away. "Whatever you have to say, I don't want to hear it. I'm no longer a part of your pack. That was *your* decision."

I turn to Callan and offer a tearful smile. "But if you'll have me, I'm a part of yours. That's *my* decision."

A victorious grin spreads across his face, and he grabs me up in a crushing hug that knocks all the breath out of me. He smashes his mouth down on mine and then pulls back, grinning. "Hell fuckin' yeah," he says. "There's not a single wolf in the world we'd rather have."

I smile up at him, my belly and chest filling with pride. No one forced me to join their pack or forced me to leave. Axel may not have used his wolf dominance on me, but these men never made me join them to begin with, and they never cast me out. Callan and Ethan welcomed me from the start. Warrick may have grudgingly taken me in, and he's grumpy and stubborn, but like the others, he let me be exactly who I am. He never once tried to make me something else, even when he used his dominance to keep peace. And most of all, he never hurt me.

Callan sets me back on my feet and swaggers toward his bike, his huge paw engulfing my small hand, his enormous frame dwarfing mine. I feel light and free, like I might burst into laughter at any moment. I don't have to be told where to sit this time. I climb on the Queen seat behind Callan, and spare one last glance in Axel's direction before we take off, spitting gravel.

He's already gone.

The smile slips from my face, just a little, and a twist of pain burrows into my heart. I wonder if the rejection ever stops hurting.

Chapter Twenty-Two

Luna

A sense of deep contentment rolls through me as I sit with my arms wrapped around Callan, zipping over the wet, cracked roads and streets of civilized Jacksonville. The sensation changes to ecstasy as we head up the long sand and dirt driveway to their—*our*—house.

He said it was my home, too.

Callan keeps one arm pressed to mine, driving with only one hand as if he's afraid of losing me again. Once parked, I climb off the Queen's seat and wait for Callan to climb off. When he does, he throws his arm around me and guides me to the house. I'm so happy I think I'll float off into the mosquito filled air like a piece of thistledown.

Inside the house, Warrick and Ethan stand from their seats at the kitchen table when we walk in.

"Luna," Ethan says, a big smile cracking over his face and showing off that adorable gap where he's missing a tooth. "You came home."

He holds out his arms, and my feet come untethered from the floor, and I leap into his arms. He kisses me hard on the mouth and then sets me on my feet. I turn to Warrick, flutters building in my belly. I'm too nervous to throw myself in his arms, especially when they're not held out to welcome me.

"Warrick," I say quietly. We stare at each other a long minute, his dark, gold-flecked eyes taking me in. For once, he doesn't frown, and his gaze is inviting rather than dominating.

"I got something to say to you—to *all* of you." My heart is positively trembling now. I glance at Callan and Ethan before returning my gaze to Warrick. I take a deep breath and go on. "I never wanted to come between you. I respect your bonds with one another. I'm sorry to have brought so much conflict into this fine home. Please don't fight over me because I can't bear that burden on my shoulders. Don't make me choose between you from one day to the next. I like all of you, and I don't want to pick one over the other and stir up jealousy. If you let me stay with your pack, I won't cause any more trouble,

I promise." I crouch before Warrick and place my palms on his boots, showing him that I'll defer to his dominance just as his brothers do. He is my Alpha.

Warrick growls. "Get your ass up, girl. Don't display your submission to me. That's not what I want right now and not what any of us want. We don't want a little bitch to bow at our feet. You're equal to any of us, Luna—and then some."

His warm hands hook beneath my arms, and he urges me to rise. I do, my head spinning. Even though Warrick's the Alpha here and the only one to openly use a dominance display to put us in line, if I stare into the eyes of his brothers too long, I know they're more dominant, too. I don't know how I could be any of their equal, let alone more.

I lift my gaze as Warrick sweeps his hand toward the chair opposite him. "Sit," he says to me. "Boys, sit."

After we've all assumed our places around the tiny square table, we all direct our attention to Warrick.

He drums his fingers on the wood surface. Then, he retrieves his pouch of tobacco and rolling papers from his pocket, spreads out a piece of paper, and sprinkles tobacco leaves on top.

As he rolls his cigarette—something he explained to me when I asked—none of us speak. Warrick lights it and takes a long drag, releasing the plume of blueish smoke over his head. "Get me an ashtray, will you, Callan?"

Callan rises, heads to the cupboard, and retrieves a small, chipped bowl. He sets it before Warrick, pours coffee into the three cups on the table, and then adds one in front of me before resuming his seat. My heart swells with the warm feeling of home. I get the same coffee, the same kind of random mug, the same as any of them.

Warrick taps the ash from the end of his smoke before balancing the cigarette on the ashtray's rim. "It's true you brought conflict between my brothers."

He directs his dark gaze at me before picking up his cigarette and taking another pull on the smoke. As he exhales, he goes on. "We've always lived together, just the three of us, since we've been old enough to call ourselves men. And I'm man enough to admit we were pretty damn lousy at dealing with the addition of a woman."

I take a tiny sip of my coffee, peeking at him over the rim.

"When you left the other night, my brothers were pissed," Warrick goes on. "I admit I was a little relieved. I don't like the chaos. It's my home, and I want to be able to kick back and relax. But as they pointed out, just because I'm the Alpha, that doesn't mean it's only *my* home. It's their home, too. And sometime in the last month, it became yours, too. So I told Callan if he could track your ass down, you could come on home and stay."

I sit at the edge of my seat, waiting for him to speak again. When he nods at me and takes another drag on his cigarette, I smile. "Thank you. I appreciate the chance to prove myself. No more chaos. I promise."

His eyes meet the eyes of each of his brothers before coming back to me. "And we agreed that none of us will touch you again of our own choosing. If anyone breaks this rule, they'll be out on their ass. It's up to Luna and Luna alone if she wants to go to one of you. Understood?"

Callan and Ethan nod solemnly. Ethan raises both hands and mutters, "Hands off."

Warrick turns back to me, his gaze penetrating mine. "If you want one of my brothers, it has to be your decision and your move, Luna. There won't be argument or conflict about it. No sneaking around behind each other's backs. The decision will be final, and we'll all respect it."

I nod, too. "I understand."

Warrick stands, picks up his smoke between his fingers, gives us a final nod, and takes his coffee to the front porch.

I sit in silence with the others, overwhelmed by the impossible choice in front of me. Both men are wonderful, but they're not the same. I want what they both offer.

Callan is kind and patient, takes me into the woods and gathers plants and set traps with me, stops and looks when I point out dragonflies circling the water. He taught me to cook and always gives me a reassuring smile and says it's delicious even when it tastes all wrong. He makes a deep, aching warmth grow in my belly when he takes my hand and gives it a gentle squeeze for no reason.

Ethan laughs while he teaches me, letting me know it's okay to mess up, that it's okay to laugh when I make a mistake. He winks at me when his brothers aren't looking, like we're in on a little secret. One rough touch of his calloused hand on my elbow or hip makes me know everything is okay. And he gave me that bliss in the bathtub like nothing I've ever felt except from Axel, and that time was followed by pain. With Ethan, there's no pain.

How can I ever make a decision when I want both of these men equally?

Chapter Twenty-Three

Luna

The guys are between jobs, so we all stay home for the rest of the day. Things are relaxed but subdued and quiet. I wonder if they're all waiting for me to choose. It sits funny in my belly, having the power in this dynamic, the power of this choice. It's up to me. No one is making choices for me anymore, saying I'll be their mate and part of their pack, or that I'm no longer their mate or part of their pack. It's up to me.

I don't like the weight of it on me. I don't want to draw it out, make them worry and wonder and want. I don't want to make either of them jealous of the other. After lying awake for an hour going back and forth about what to do, I know I'm never going to sleep with the decision hanging over my head. I have to make it now.

So, I do.

In the dark of night, I slip from beneath my covers, ease out the door of the bedroom and tiptoe across the hall. I've never been inside Warrick's lair—I was always too scared before. But tonight, I step past the threshold of his door and head for his slumbering form. Quietly, I crawl beneath his covers and press my naked body to his massive back.

He startles, then relaxes and stays quiet for a few minutes.

Did I make the wrong choice? Warrick said I could choose, but maybe he didn't mean him. He told me to choose between his brothers. Maybe I'm not supposed to choose the Alpha. Maybe an Alpha makes his own choice, dominates his mate into submission.

After a few minutes, he sighs and rolls onto his back. "What are you doing here, baby girl?"

"Do you want me to leave?" I ask, biting at my lip.

His large hand lands on my thigh, his calloused palm covering my soft skin. "No."

I cuddle closer to his body, and a soft growl rumbles through his giant form.

"I've always admired you, Warrick," I say, caressing the soft hairs that cover his powerful chest. "You're everything an

Alpha should be. You're so strong, and you only want what's right for your brothers. You put them in their place when they need it, but you set aside your own needs and wants if it serves the pack."

"What needs and wants?" he says, rolling to face me.

His enormous cock lands on my leg, hard and hot against my cool, bare skin. My core trembles, and I swallow hard.

In the dim moonlight, I trace the outline of his shoulders, as wide as an ogre's and twice as strong, running my fingers down the scars on them to his broad, muscular chest. "I think you want me," I whisper, my voice barely audible.

He only grunts, but his cock throbs against my thigh in response.

"Don't you?" I ask, my heart racing like a swamp rabbit. Did I get it all wrong?

"Luna…"

I lay my small, soft hand on the rough stubble of his cheek. "You're the kind of man who would never step on the toes of your brothers to take what you want. So, I'm giving it to you. If…" I break off, swallowing the trembling, liquidy ache in my throat. "If you'll have me."

"I haven't even been nice to you," he points out. "Why would you want me?"

"You say that, and maybe you'd like me to believe it, but we both know I'm here because you allow it. You took me to town and let me pick my own clothes, my own hair. You don't try to teach me things to make me like you. You just let me be exactly what I want to be. You treat me like a part of your pack. You might not talk as much as the others, but I see you, Warrick. You put my needs before yours, too. You had every right to claim me as Alpha and end the discussion, but you didn't. You let me make the choice. And I choose to give you what you need, to put you first for once."

"Oh, fuck, baby girl," he says, adding a wry chuckle. "You're everything I need and everything I don't need all rolled into one fuckable little piece of ass. You're damn sure the one thing that's going to get me killed."

I suck in a breath. "Killed?"

"Yeah, baby-girl. Killed." His thick arm circles my waist, bringing me flush against him as he nuzzles my neck. "But is that going to stop me?"

I clutch his mountainous shoulders, my insides trembling with fear and heat as he pushes his hips against mine, the iron ridge of his cock crushing into the soft place between my legs that Ethan shaved. Is he going to do what Axel did? Will it hurt that much?

"If I were a decent man, I'd let you find someone your own age who isn't a criminal," he murmurs, pulling my leg over his hip.

"I don't want a decent man." This new sense of power coursing through me is a heady elixir, but also a bit terrifying. "I want *you*."

"The devil help us, then. I'm going to wreck you, baby girl."

"If that's what you want," I breathe. "I'm yours. Do what you want to me."

I rock my hips against him, letting him feel how wet I am. He lets out a low, deep rumble of pleasure, so I do it again. My core throbs, aching to be filled. I can feel the power thrumming through his veins, but he doesn't move. He lets me move, sliding along his length until I reach the thick, rounded end that's as wet as me. He smells of musk and pure male wolf. I whimper with desire.

In one swift move, he rolls me on top of him. His cock stands rigidly between us, swollen, lined with thick, throbbing veins. In rhythm with his next sigh, he strokes his calloused hands along my sides and traces my waist and my hips. Then, he palms the front of my thighs all the way from my knees to my bare skin that Ethan called a pussy. He tugs the lips open with his thumbs, spreading them further open against his shaft.

His hands are sure and firm as he caresses me, keeping his gaze pinned to me as he leisurely explores my body and then returns to the swollen bud that Ethan took so much time on, the one that made me explode. I moan and rock against his erection, taking pleasure in his hard cock against my slick, wet core.

This elicits a low chuckle from him, which vibrates through me. He seizes my hips and slows down my grinding movements. "Easy, baby girl. It's been a while for this old man."

A breathy laugh escapes me. "You're not old, Warrick."

"I feel old," he says, releasing my hips and spreading his hands over my tiny breasts. "Fuck, please tell me you're eighteen."

"I'm eighteen," I agree.

"I'm twice your age," he growls. "I feel like a fucking pervert wanting to fuck you as raw and hard as I'm about to."

He pinches my nipples, and both sharp pain and searing pleasure flood my core. I let my head fall back and moan.

"Sweet fucking Jesus, woman." His fingers keep tweaking my hard buds, followed by soft caresses. Then, more pain, and again, more sweet pleasure. I didn't know pain could feel good, but when he gives it, it's so mixed up with the pleasure I can't tell them apart. I grind myself helplessly along his hard length, needing relief so badly I think I'll burst.

At last Warrick grabs my hips, and I feel his will crush down on me, pinning me in place. "Stop," he orders. "I don't want to come yet."

I worry my bottom lip with my teeth, cowering as I stop my frantic movement. I want the experience I had with Ethan, but with Warrick. But I must have done something wrong.

"Don't you want to bury your cock inside me?" I whisper.

Warrick's cock throbs, and a drop of whitish liquid oozes out onto his wall of abs. He moves his thumb against that bud that makes me feel like I'll burst like a comet overhead, and it's all I can do not to move against him and find relief.

"Please," I whisper, panting for it.

"I don't want to hurt you," he says.

"How do you know if it will hurt me?"

"Have you seen me?" he says with a chuckle. "I haven't found a woman who could take me in too fucking long. This is going to hurt, baby girl, no doubt about it."

I lean forward, resting my hands on his mountainous muscles. My lilac hair drapes across his torso, and he closes his eyes and draws a long breath. I drag my hair down his inked skin before tossing it back and looking straight into his eyes. "Mate me, Warrick. I don't care if it hurts."

"Fuck," he growls, rolling over on top of me and knocking my knees apart with his. He pushes the slippery head of his cock to my slick flesh. "Don't say I didn't warn you."

"Warn me?"

"I'm going to fuck you so hard you can't breathe, baby girl. You're *mine*. I'm going to fucking breed you. And you're going to love it."

I nod eagerly, wincing when I feel the strain of his huge size trying to fit inside my tiny opening. He holds himself up on his hands, his body suspended over mine, with just our hips pressed together. His shoulders are twice as wide as mine, and I have to look up to find his face, since my eyes are only up to his chest. My body feels tiny and helpless as I lay under his looming hugeness. His eyes pin mine, and I can feel his dominance rolling over me, almost pinning me to the bed. I want to please him so bad it hurts, to do exactly what he commands. It's a desperate feeling, but also one that I know will make me feel more rewarded than anything I've ever done.

"Spread yourself open for your Alpha," he growls.

I spread my legs as wide as they'll go and reach down, pulling my pussy open with both hands. Warrick looks down at what I'm doing and groans, his hips thrusting forward with a quick jerk. I cry out as he breaches my entrance and the sting of being stretched burns through me.

"Holy mother of the devil himself, you're so fucking tight," he growls. "You still feel like a virgin."

"Keep going," I say through panting breaths. "Please, Warrick. I need you. I need to give myself to you. Take me.

Claim me. Show my body it's yours." From my mating with Axel, I know the worst pain is yet to come. But the ache in my core urges me to go on, anyway.

"Oh, I'm going to keep going," he assures me, his body coiled with power. "That was just the head. You got a long way to go, baby girl. And Daddy's going to give it all to you, because you're damn right. Your body is mine, and I'm going to show you just how good that feels."

He unleashes some of that power, driving in another few inches. My breath catches, and I blink away tears. I feel like he's going to rip me open, but when I lift my head to look down, he's only halfway in. I drop my head back, gasping for breath.

"You're doing great, baby girl," he says. "Just relax and let Daddy in."

Warmth spreads through me at his words, and I feel safe and cared for as he waits for me to adjust, not moving a muscle while my walls unclench from his massive cock. When I nod, he rolls his hips forward, stretching me wider than even Axel did. A tear slips from the corner of my eye, and my knees curl up. "Oh, god," I gasp. "I'm not sure…"

"You can take it," he says, gently swiping his tongue over my cheek, wiping my tear away. "Daddy wants to see every inch of his cock buried in his baby girl. Don't you want to see that?"

I bob my head, biting my lip. He waits until I relax, then kisses my forehead gently. "This is the last one. You want to watch?"

When I nod, he folds the second pillow and lifts my shoulders, putting it under me so I can watch without craning my neck. Then he pushes the rest of the way inside me. I whimper, another tear escaping. I'm stretched so far I think my flesh might tear, and deep inside me aches where he's pushed up against my insides. But it's not just painful. The pleasure of it builds, almost overwhelming me.

"You ready for Daddy to fuck you senseless, baby girl?" I nod, but he grabs my chin, forcing my gaze to his. "Say it."

"I'm ready."

"Tell me," he commands. "All of it."

"Fuck me senseless, Daddy."

Warrick begins to move then, stroking my hair as he pulls back and pushes back in, his thrusts hard and deep until I can't stop the helpless whimpers from spilling from my lips. I'm so full I think I'll burst, and I can't tell where pain stops and pleasure begins. I only know I want him inside me forever.

His eyes lock on mine, and I feel his power over me looming like his body. "Not a sound out of you," he growls. "I own this orgasm—it's mine."

I nod frantically, biting my lips together.

"Get on your hands and knees."

My brow furrows in confusion, but I comply, aching for him to fill me again the moment he pulls out, covered in our fragrant juices. He crouches behind me, easing his cock inside me from behind. "Daddy wants his baby girl to finger her pussy while her fucks her from behind," he says, guiding one of my hands between my legs, to the place Ethan stroked before.

"What do I do?" I ask.

"Rub your clit until you come on my cock."

I do as I'm told, matching his rhythm as Warrick pumps inside of me. Pleasure builds until I can't hold it back. I open my lips to cry out, then suck the sound back in. Somehow, holding it in magnifies the sensations in my body, and the ache deep in my core can't take it. It explodes inside me like an earthquake ripping me apart, and I cry out helplessly. Warrick's hand reaches around and clamps over my mouth, and he bites down on my neck, thrusting faster and harder, until it happens again.

He growls and gives one final, brutal thrust, and I feel a stab of pain as he stretches me wider, and then hot liquid gushes into my core. I explode again, even though I'm so wrung out I'm sobbing and shaking with the intensity. I bite his fingers to keep from making a sound as wave after wave of ecstatic pleasure courses through my limbs a third time. I'm trembling so hard I can't hold myself up any longer. At last I collapse, pressing the side of my head into his musky pillow as Warrick holds me pinned, his cock throbbing and jerking inside me as he squeezes more liquid into my heat. At last, he withdraws from me and rolls by my side.

"Good girl," he whispers, wrapping his huge body protectively around me, stroking my hair and kissing my head as I drift into the ethers, floating on a sea of satisfaction I never dreamed was possible.

Chapter Twenty-Four

Warrick

I can't fucking sleep. Luna's curled up next to me like a little pup, and I just had the best damn sex of my life, but sleep won't come for me tonight. Yeah, she chose me, and I'm fucking flattered, but I took something both Ethan and Callan wanted—after I ripped into them for touching her. I figured if I kept my distance and gave her my surly side, she'd want nothing to do with me. But here she came, a naked little waif in the night, slipping between my sheets and saying things to me in her wide-eyed innocence that no man could resist. Hell, she probably didn't even know how half of that sounded to my ears.

I drag my hand through my hair and kick the covers off. I imagine what that asshole Axel would do if he knew I took his sloppy seconds and made her a queen. Ten years ago, I challenged him for dominance and lost, but tonight, I got my vindication. Tonight, I didn't just touch his mate like my brothers did. I fucked her raw and deep, shaping her cunt to *my* measure.

I fucking *claimed* every inch of her. Instead of pulling out at the last minute and coming all over her back, like I usually do, I shot my seed inside her while seizing her neck between my teeth. She submitted to my claim, and I rewarded her by making her come over and over, lifting her up where he cut her down. I run my fingers across the scar on her skin, and she shivers in her sleep and cuddles closer.

"Luna," I say, nudging her with my elbow.

"Mm-hmm?" she says in a sleepy sounding voice.

"Baby girl, you can't stay here. Go on back to your room now."

"Why?" she says, rubbing her eyes with her fists. She looks so goddamned sweet my cock starts to twitch, eager for another round inside that slippery little vice between her thighs.

"I gotta work out some things with Callan and Ethan," I tell her. "It wouldn't look right if they found you here."

"I thought you said it was my choice."

"It is," I say, sweeping a strand of her colorful hair back. "I just never considered you might choose me. After I called them off, they'd be pissed that I went ahead and took you for myself."

Her nose scrunches up, and she looks at me like I've sprouted wings. "Why wouldn't I come to you? I like you. *All* of you."

"I know, baby girl," I say, stroking her cheek. "But it'll look like I chose, like I pulled the Alpha card to get you on your back. Like it wasn't your choice."

"It *was* my choice," she says, laying her small hand on my rough cheek.

And I should be on my knees thanking the devil himself for that, because hearing her call me Daddy and then fucking the tightest pussy I've ever felt in my life was just about the best thing I've ever done. My gaze drops to her mouth, and fuck if I don't want to taste it, and fuck it, and…

"Okay, I'll go," she says, sitting up and stretching when I don't answer. The sheet falls down around her waist, and her little tits rise in the moonlight. I'm so fucking hard I'd tell her I changed my mind if I didn't see her wincing when she sat up.

As tight as she was, she's going to be walking bowlegged for days after taking that pounding.

On silent feet, she pads to the door, then turns back to look at me over her shoulder. I just about blow my load all over again, but she gives me a shy little wave and disappears before I can order her back to the bed and see if that mouth feels as good as it looks.

When she's gone, I have to jerk off just to get the image out of my head. Then I lie awake, staring out the window and thinking how fucking long it's been since I lay awake thinking about a woman. Since I left home and didn't have to worry about our mama, that's how long.

A sound outside my window startles me—a soft rustling followed by a dull thwack. Even though there are plenty of swamp critters, I'm on guard when I don't smell any kind of animal. I drop off the bed and head outside to check the perimeter.

In the dim light of dawn, I catch a faint glimmer of metal and a white square affixed to a tree at the edge of the yard. I scent the air, but no one is nearby, so I hurry over to investigate.

I keep my ears pricked and my nose on alert, though, in case this is an attempt at an ambush.

A fighting knife still quivers in the bark of the old hickory. I yank down the paper and read the scrawled letters.

Give the bitch up tonight, or you'll all die.

My blood turns to ice, and a big grin spreads across my face. Oh, I like the sound of that challenge. Whoever issued this threat has a death wish.

I scent the air again, and then I head inside to put the coffee on. I don't bother with clothes. I won't be fighting in human form, and busting out of them when I shift is a pain in the ass. Then I sit on the porch and roll a cigarette, watching dawn creep into the sky. I'm almost done with my smoke when I catch the first scent. I can smell both vampires and wolves.

I toss my cigarette and rub my hands together—this is going to be good.

Tipping back my head, I issue a few wolf yips. A minute later, Callan and Ethan stumble out onto the porch.

"What is it?" Callan says. "You're up early."

I hand them the paper that was pinned to the tree.

"Fuck," Ethan says, punching a fist into his palm. "We just got her back. Who tracked us?"

"No one had to track us," I say. "We're not hiding her. We welcomed her, and she accepted."

"They can come through the three of us if they want her," Callan says, an edge of ferocity in his voice.

I can't wait to exact blood for this threat on Luna's life, but I keep my cool.

"Nothing to do now but have our coffee and wait for the bastards to show their faces."

When we step inside, Luna comes padding into the kitchen on bare feet, her hair sticking out in five different directions, looking hot as hell itself in a baggy t-shirt and bare legs.

"What's going on?" she asks, rubbing her eyes. "I heard y'all talking outside."

"There's been a threat on your life."

She eyes the paper and frowns.

I want to eat the heart of the man who caused her pain. If this came from Axel, I'll be all too happy to tell him I filled his True Mate's womb with my seed—right before I rip his head off.

"Come here, baby girl," I say, patting my thigh.

She minces across the room and sits on my knee, casting a beguiling gaze at each of us with those big eyes. "I brought more conflict," she whispers.

"None of that," I say, squeezing her hip. "You're part of the pack. We fight for our own. You're ours now, and we're not letting you go."

Tears well up in her baby blue eyes. "Thank you."

I turn to my brothers. They deserve the truth, and they deserve it coming from my mouth.

"Luna came to my room last night," I say. "I fucked her good and hard."

Callan nods. "As you should."

Ethan smiles and takes a drink of coffee. "That's our Alpha. Taking what's yours."

"Alright then," I say, standing. I can smell the ashy dead smell of vamps coming closer. I'm ready to fight side by side with my brothers to save the woman who changed us all in the short time we've known her. "Let's win this fight. For Luna."

Chapter Twenty-Five

Luna

Fog hangs heavy and expectant in the woods surrounding the triplet's house. There's an eeriness to the sounds of crickets and frogs singing their dawn songs that sends chills rippling across my skin. A bird adds its piercing cry at random intervals. It stirs a sense of foreboding I can't kick from my bloodstream. Someone wants me dead. But who? Why?

"Get on back in the house, Luna," Warrick commands me, giving my bottom a little squeeze. We're sitting on the porch swing while Callan stands on one of the support posts and Ethan sits on the step. "We're going to kill whatever assholes posted this warning, but you need to be inside, out of harm's way."

I lean back on his knee, arms folded over my chest. "You said we were a pack. If you fight, I fight. It's as simple as that."

The triplets look back and forth between each other, sending their secret messages that I don't understand, not having grown up with them.

"You listen here," I say, not appreciating being kept out of a decision about myself. I've had enough of that to last a lifetime. "I'm not a puppy. I'm a full-grown wolf, same as y'all. They said you had to give me up, which means this is my fight. If you want to fight by my side, I'm honored to have each and every one of you, but you can't cut me out. I'm going to fight to stay here, and if you fight to keep me here, too, then I'll just love y'all all the more for it."

I chose Warrick tonight, but that doesn't mean he's the only one I love. I realized that when I lay thinking on it last night, trying to decide. I'm fighting to stay not just with Warrick but with all of them. And just because I chose him last night, that doesn't mean I'll choose him every night. But that's a conversation for another time, when the smell of vampire isn't drifting into the clearing in front of the house.

A branch snaps nearby, and Warrick straightens, already on alert. He makes a gesture with his hand, and Callan and Ethan nod.

Another crack snaps into the air.

Warrick slides me off his lap and stands, popping his knuckles and grinning. "It's been too quiet lately, boys. Let's go smash some skulls." He heads down the steps, the others close on his heel. I follow, feeling more scared than brave, though I'm not about to let it show.

Outside, as dawn washes the darkness from the sky, several men emerge from the woods, carrying bats and metal bars.

Warrick grins wider. "Vampires," he confirms in a low growl, since he probably thinks I don't know the scent yet. "You know what to do, boys."

"Go for the heart or the head," Ethan says. "Get some blood to make us stronger as we fight." He spits on the ground and then punches his fist into his other palm.

"Baby girl," Warrick says, glancing over his shoulder. "You stay behind me if you need to. I'll be your cover. Whatever you do, stay safe."

"I got this," I say, puffing out my chest.

"Yeah, you do," Callan says, chuckling and affectionately ruffling my hair. "We'll get 'em, pet."

"Let's move," Warrick says.

As one, my three men shift into wolves and race toward the vampires. I shift, too, but I pause for a moment, studying their attack. I'm not skilled in fighting anything but catfish and an occasional gator, and I don't want to get myself killed or act without strategy and get the men killed. They fight as one, though their attack seems simple enough. They avoid the bats and bars, lunge for the male's necks, and tear their heads off with their sharp teeth and powerful jaws.

Callan shifts back to human, seizes one of the bats, and swings it overhead, bringing it down on an injured male's ribcage. "Here you go, Warrick. Eat your fill!"

The ribcage splits open with a sickening crunch. Blood spews from the opening. For every vampire they take down, a handful more appear. They leap onto Warrick's back, moving so fast they're a blur as they slash and bite, barrel into the wolves, and beat them with their metal weapons. One of them charges into Ethan and sends him tumbling across the clearing when he goes for the dead vampire's heart. Seeming unfazed, Callan proceeds to the next downed vampire. Grabbing one of the metal bars from the ground, he plunges it straight through the guy's heart with such force that blood and organ bits shoot into the air.

"This one's mine," he roars, thrusting his hand into the chest cavity and seizing the bloody heart. He tears it apart with his teeth. Another vampire rushes toward Callan, the bat in his hands at the ready.

I want to scream, "Look out!" but I'm in wolf form, so only a woof comes out. Callan spins my way and sees the guy coming in for an attack. In a blur, he shifts back to wolf and leaps at the vampire, knocking him to the ground.

I'm half their size as a wolf as well as a human, but I'm still bigger than the vampires. I lunge for one and clamp my teeth down on his throat, the way I see Warrick doing. I brace my paws against him, shake my head and rip out chunks his neck until he goes limp. He falls to the ground, and a sense of pride fills my chest. It feels good to be a part of this fight.

A force like a tree flying in a hurricane slams into my side, sending me sprawling. I howl and jump to my feet, swiping at the vampire. She grins and ducks aside when I charge her again. Then she leaps onto my back, her arms wrapping around my neck in a stranglehold. I howl, and a second later, Ethan lands beside us in a single bound and rips her from my back, sending her head rolling and her body sailing into the trees. I send him a silent thanks and dive for another vampire, ripping into her middle to take her out of the fight before killing her.

When I bite into her neck, I can feel her cold, dead blood run over my tongue. I want to spit it out, but I remember what the guys said. I swallow it instead, and a few minutes later, I feel the strength they promised. It's like coffee. It takes terrible, but it comes with an excited, shaky, charged feeling that runs through my blood like it did the first time I had coffee, when the guys laughed at me when I freaked out after drinking a full cup. But they were nice, too, and Callan took me for a run in the woods to help get the energy out.

Now, the way to get energy out is to kill. Mama taught me that you should only kill to survive. In the swamp, that meant killing something to eat. Even when we killed one of the poisonous snakes that would slither under the walls, we always ate it. Out here, it's no different. I kill so that I can live, and if I eat a little of the kill, it's all the more justified.

There are so many of them, but we're winning. They keep coming out of the woods, but the stream of reinforcements has died to a trickle. I've killed a handful of vamps, and many more bodies litter the clearing. Ethan is feasting on a screaming woman while Warrick tears the head off another vampire while two more cling to his back. Callan has gone into the woods a bit, but I hear the snarling and see pieces of vampires flying through the air as he tears them apart. There's blood everywhere. It bathes the stones and the sand and spatters across the tree trunks. It coats the bushes and the leaves which lay scattered across the ground.

I'm pumped with adrenaline and vampire blood, ready to take down my next victim. I start for a short male, but he sprints into the woods when he sees me coming. I give chase. I'm just behind the house, diving for the man under a sprawling oak, when something heavy falls over my body. I stumble, caught in folds of rope, trying to figure out what happened. It's a net! Wrestling and snarling, I struggle to get free. I shift into my human form and claw at the netting, searching for a knot to untie so I can climb free.

Strong arms wrap around me from behind and lift me in the air. A male laughs quietly as I squirm and kick in his embrace. "You're a feisty one, aren't you?" he says in a familiar voice.

It's Evan, the bastard who tricked me into thinking he was a friend and then stole wolf secrets from me while I was drugged. The man responsible for the ache in my heart and the shame in my blood that never goes away. He's the reason I was banished from Axel's pack, the reason he severed our bond.

I start to scream, but he slaps his palm over my mouth. I try to bite him through the net, but the webbing prevents me from connecting with his flesh. I start to shift back into a wolf, but before I can, something sharp and quick bites into my hip. It's small but deep, like a honey locust thorn I got lodged in my calf one time. Evan chuckles, the sound oily and sinister in my ear.

"Don't go wolfing out on me," he says. "That's no way to have a conversation. Plus, you smell so much better as a human than a mangy, wet dog."

Two other vampires rush from the woods in our direction, calling in whispers to each other. I struggle and kick, whatever I can to get free, but it's useless. I feel groggy like I did after drinking his water, my limbs uncoordinated. I call to my wolf to help, but she's even more disoriented than I am, and I can't seem to remember how to pull her forward to take over.

A female vamp cuts the net free, and Evan tosses me over his shoulder. We start moving, so fast it makes me almost vomit the coffee I had this morning. The wind blows into my nose so hard I can't breathe, like when I was on Warrick's bike and stuck my head around him to see. Trees and marshes blur by so fast I can hardly make them out. Suddenly, we skid to a halt beside an orange van.

My heart sinks into the ground like an anvil.

The vampires bind the netting around my ankles and gag me with a foul-smelling cloth that makes my eyes burn and water. I'm deposited on the hard floor of the van and guarded by the largest of the three vampires, a scary looking male with no hair on his head, eyeglasses, and the longest fangs I've ever seen.

Evan disappears and reappears in the driver's seat.

The van tears out of the swamp and along a dirt road. Only when we turn onto a smooth road does the scary guy yank off my gag. I wiggle my jaw back and forth, trying to get some feeling back in my face. "What do you want from me?" I demand, though my voice sounds shaky and scared. "I don't taste good to vampires, and my blood does nothing for y'all."

"And yet, you partook in ours so greedily," Evan purrs from the front seat.

Scary Guy laughs. In the dim light in the back of the van, his face is lined with shadows, making him look even more sinister. "We don't want to eat you, mutt."

"Yes," says the woman. "We require your services for other reasons."

"What kind of reasons? You got a problem with the triplets?" I tug against the restraints binding my arms and legs.

"Those outlaws?" Evan scoffs. "They have no power, so they're of no use to us. They were simply an inconvenience that had to be dealt with, sweet Luna. You, though…"

"*I* have no power!" I blurt out. "Please let me go. I'm just one lone wolf. What can you want with me?"

Evan chuckles again, that sound that slithers down my back like a snake hanging from the ceiling. "You're a bargaining chip. We can use you for leverage with the Jacksonville pack."

A bitter laugh escapes my lips. "Good luck with that. I ain't Axel's mate no more. He don't want nothing to do with me. He's the one who threw me away, made me a lone wolf. That's why I found other lone wolves like me."

"Hmm," Evan says, sounding amused. "You really are innocent, aren't you, Luna?"

"He severed the True Mate bond!" I insist. I twist around to show the scary vampire the pale pink scar on my arm. "Look, the mark don't lie. We're not mates. He'll never negotiate to get me back."

"I wouldn't be so sure about that." Scary-guy grins. Every tooth is pointed and sharp, as if he's ground them into tiny daggers.

"You're never going to get anywhere with the Jacksonville pack if all you have to bargain with is me."

Scary-guy's expression darkens, and he stares at me through slits.

"You honestly don't know, do you?"

Evan makes that horrid laugh again. "Oh, sweet Luna. Who do you think destroyed your little shack in Bogbeast Waters?"

"I—I don't know," I say. "Are you saying you did that?"

This time, the woman throws her head back and laughs. Then she twists around in the front seat to look at me, her eyes shining with amusement. "No, honey. Axel destroyed it, so you'd have nowhere to go. He was counting on you running back to him."

His words land like an arrow in my heart. Axel destroyed my home? I blink rapidly, fighting back the tears. It can't be true. It's bad enough that he tore my soul to shreds. Wanting me to come back to him after that seems even more cruel. It can't be true. I close my eyes and try not to feel the sickening speed of the van or think about the vampires' cruel words and laughter.

They're lying. Axel doesn't want me. If he wanted me, he would have showed it when he had me.

Chapter Twenty-Six

Luna

The van screeches to a stop, and I tumble against the driver's seat, still bound by ropes and a net.

"How do you know that?" I mumble once I've managed to right myself somewhat. "How do you know Axel destroyed my home and still wants me? He severed our bond…"

"It's easy," Evan says, throwing open his door. He comes around to the back of the van and drags me out by my feet. The uneven, corrugated metal floor collides with my backside. Throwing me over his shoulder as effortlessly as if I'm a dead swamp rabbit, he continues to talk as he strides away from the vehicle. "The True Mate bond isn't something a wolf takes lightly. Axel might have gone through the motions of breaking the bond, but there's no way he could sever the connection completely. It's impossible."

The sweet scent of a creek fills my nostrils, and I recognize Evan's place even while upside down.

"I swear to you—we're *not* True Mates anymore," I say, bouncing along his back. But even as I say the words, I know they're not true. The bond was broken, but it can't change what we are. I can still sense the energetic bindings, which were once as tight as the ropes cinching me. Now they're cut loose, like two ends of a rope blowing in the wind. Only now the ropes represent rage and betrayal instead of love and safety. That's why my wolf cries every time we even think of him. Whatever bound us was severed, but it's never truly gone, like ugly scar tissue where healthy flesh once lived.

"We'll see," Evan says, sounding unconcerned.

Evan's footsteps are accompanied by the other vampires who accosted me. He steps through a doorway and tosses me onto a plush rug. "Untie her," he commands to one of the other vampires.

The woman approaches me and pulls a sharp knife from a leather holder on her belt. I wince, hoping the knife doesn't carve me to pieces. Once freed, I rub my chafed arms and legs. "Are you letting me go?"

"Ha! Good one," Evan says. "No, darling, we're going to put you somewhere safe." He inclines his head toward the scary one and then saunters away.

The woman seizes my wrist with her leather-gloved hand and drags me back outside.

"Where are you taking me?" I say, tugging my wrist against her formidable grip. I'm still a little woozy from whatever they stuck me with, but if I can break free, I can hide and wait it out until I can shift.

"To your kennel." She grins, revealing beautiful white teeth bordered by fangs.

I struggle as we approach a gleaming new cage set in the center of the yard, but my human form is no match for a vampire. She shoves me inside and slams the door shut. Then she fishes a key out of her pocket and fits it inside a sturdy lock, securing the cage. Without another word, she wiggles her fingers in a teasing little wave, pivots, and heads back toward the front door.

My fingers curl around the metal bars, but I yank them back when my skin burns upon contact. I let out a yelp and shake my blistered hands, staring down at my palms. I didn't feel any heat coming from the bars at all, but my skin is burned and searing with pain.

She-Vamp pauses at the door. "Oh. Did I forget to tell you your kennel is made of silver? I hear that's like an electric fence to a wolf. Am I right?"

"Asshole," I mutter before sucking on the blisters.

She laughs and disappears inside the house.

I sink down on the floor of the cage but immediately leap up when the bars burn my bottom. I can stand between the bars so I don't touch the silver, but I can't sit. I'm drowsy and wired at the same time. Every movement is slow and makes me sway dizzily, but I'm wide awake and still wired from the vampire blood. I wait for them to come back, but no one emerges from the house.

All day, I wait. I don't dare approach the bars that surround me as I'm still licking my blistered skin. I watch dragonflies and butterflies flit outside my cage, landing briefly on the foliage and then flying away. I study the trees that stretch their leafy arms into the sky. I even regard the sky itself with its endless blue, sometimes punctuated by drifting clouds. The heat makes me drowsy, but I can't sit. I shift from one foot to the other, then crouch, then kneel, gaining a blister on the inside of my knee when I get to close to the silver.

Occasionally a car, truck, or motorcycle drives up and parks. Each time, I jump to my feet, hoping one of the triplets will appear. They'd never give up on me.

If they're alive...

I won't think of that. It's always another vampire coming to see Evan. I now know their scent well now, like bitter ash and death. They stride to the front door of the Evan's lair and disappear inside its sparkling white facade. Sometimes they point and laugh at me, but most ignore me.

By nightfall, I'm famished, thirsty, and fatigued, as my growling stomach can attest. Where are the triplets? They must be searching for me. I won't entertain other possibilities. They don't know where I am, but they'll find me. I just have to wait.

The front door opens, and a slice of light cuts through the darkness. A horde of vampires exits the house, laughing and talking.

Evan looks over at me and grins. "Nice to see you've settled in so well. You look right at home in a cage, little doggie."

If I were free, I'd tear his heart from his chest and eat it like the men do.

"Good hunting tonight, everyone!" a boar-like man says.

Another vampire says, "I hope your plan works, Drake."

The one I called Scary Guy, who must be Drake, responds. "Oh, it'll work. I've sensed him lurking about."

The hair on my neck prickles with excitement. Which of my men has come for me? Surely it's Warrick this time. After what we shared last night, he wouldn't give up on me. Why can't I scent him, though? I know each of their scents by heart at this point. They all smell of sweat and have the primal, *man* smell I never encountered until Axel. Callan also smells like the salt marshes in the hot sun, and Ethan's scent has a hint of the woods and the exhaust from his bike. Warrick smells like leather and cigarettes. But I can't find any of them in the air tonight.

Still, the idea that one of my pack is looking for me gives me hope. When the vampires depart, I shift into wolf and howl.

I call for my new lovers. I tell them, "I'm here, come and find me!" After an hour of my plaintive howls, I'm worn out and have to stop. I can only hope they got my message. I lower my head and try to sleep standing, not to think about the latest thing Axel didn't tell me—that even when our bond isn't connected to each other, it's never truly gone. He will be part of me forever, a wound that never heals.

It's still dark when I finally rouse from my half-sleep of exhaustion and sway on my feet. It's the time when the transition between night and day begins. I know it to be a time of power, when darkness yields to light.

More than that, I smell him—one lone wolf.

I stand at attention, searching the shadows for him. Is it Callan, who found me before? Or will it be Ethan this time? My skin tingles and my fur rises with excitement.

A large wolf pads out of the woods toward me, silent as a cloud moving across the moon. I step back in confusion. This is not the right wolf.

I shift into human, knowing he can't reach me inside my silver cage, since he's a wolf, too. I bare my teeth.

"Who are you?" I ask, even though I know. I don't want him to know that he's familiar to me. I want him to think he'll always be a stranger.

The wolf shifts, and once again I find myself face to face with the man who hurt me so much. He keeps showing up, refusing to let me forget.

"They put you in a silver cage?" he asks, his voice and eyes burning with dark fury.

"Why are you here?" I demand.

"I heard you calling," he says simply.

"I wasn't calling you."

He flinches, just a bit, but doesn't acknowledge that. Instead, he sighs. "I'm here to take you home."

"Your home is not mine, Axel."

He steps to the edge of the cage, wrapping his hands around the bars. I hear the hiss of his skin burning, and his jaw clenches, but he doesn't step back. He stares at me through the bars of my cage, his eyes sad and intense. "You're wrong," he says quietly. "Just like I was wrong. You're my home, Luna. And whether you like it or not, I am yours."

I step back again, wrapping my arms around myself, the wail of my wolf inside me so full of anguish I nearly crumble. "No," I say, shaking my head. "It's not true."

"It is true," he says. "I know you feel it, too. Stop running from me. You can't escape destiny."

"You're the one who tried to escape destiny," I cry, my hands balling into fists and tears filling my eyes at the fresh reminder of his betrayal. "You severed us, Axel. You wounded my wolf—my soul."

He shakes his head and steps back, his voice going flat. "You might be angry at first, but you'll thank me when you stop being proud and admit this is where you belong. Now get yourself together, Luna. I'm taking you home."

*

Go here to get Book 2:

http://books2read.com/rejectedmate2

To get updates on book 2, sneak peaks and insider info, cover reveals and more, join my B-Team Newsletter: https://www.subscribepage.com/rejected-mate .